I0737866

Dear Diary

KEVIA DAUPHINEY

Much & More
PUBLISHING

Houston, TX

Somewhere in the world, there's a mom thinking
I just want to pee as a kid tries to force its way
into the bathroom with her—this book is for her.

Dear Diary,

I am failing at life in spectacular fashion. I hate my husband, my kids are monsters, and to top it all off, I'm fat. Fatter. Fat. Doesn't matter. Today, I saw an episode of *My 600-Lb. Life*, and thought, *I could do that.* I could start eating right now and just eat myself into an early, oversized grave—urn, actually, because who wants Funeral Home Guy squeezing their extra thigh meat into a pair of white panty hose? Correction: I could easily eat myself into an early, overfilled urn.

At this point, it would probably be easier for me to make it to six hundred pounds than lose all this baby weight. Factor in my grandma's gut-to-butt ratio, the weight I gained from the DEPO shot after Kid One, and the postpartum ice cream weight after Kid Two, and you'd know I was doomed from the start. I don't even want to think about the weight loss I got

so excited about when I was breastfeeding. I kept that kick start up for a long while, only to find out I was pregnant again fifteen pounds before hitting my goal weight.

The husband claims he doesn't care about the weight gain, but I'd bet the last Snickers bar I have hidden in the laundry room that he's lying. If he'd gained forty pounds since we met, I'd be dropping hints about physical trainers and praying about divorce. But then again, I'm fairly sure I'm a horrible person. I just feel tired, busted, and disgusted. I have no idea where this is going.

P.S. I thought going to church would make me feel better, but that sucked too.

Dear Diary,

Is it wrong to get physically ill at the thought of going to church again? I'm sure some discerning saint just clutched her pearls as I wrote that. But seriously, who wants to sit through another night of revival? Last night was bad enough. The Women in the Word ladies' group is hosting a weeklong event, and I went to church thinking, *Surely, I'll be encouraged.* Wrong! I left a sink full of dishes and graham cracker crumbs in the high chair, all for the pleasure of being beat over the head with Proverbs 31. Again. The entire time I wanted to scream, "Give me a few servants, and I could do all that too!" "Do more and do it better" is not what anyone already struggling to balance their life wants or needs to hear. God, help me.

At this point, I am so dissatisfied with so many things in my life, I have come to the conclusion that it must be me. It *has* to be me. Right? They can't all

be crazy. Can they? To make it worse, I only had two dollars to put in the offering envelope. We are not even going to address how embarrassing that is. Sometimes I feel like I'm just there to get my "went to church" card punched. I'm just not feeling edified by it all. I almost feel trapped. If I choose to leave, even if it's just to find a new church home, I instantly become a good, old-fashioned, backsliding heathen. I should just quit. At least backsliding is fun. OK, God, I quit. Don't smite me. I take it back (kind of).

Dear Diary,

Today was great! OK, that may have been an over-exaggeration. I guess it was as close to great as you can get with four kids. *Almost* incident-free is all I can hope for at this point. Anywho, me and the kids actually completed our entire lesson plan for the day—every subject, every task, all neatly checked off. Why can't every day be like this? The oldest kid even asked for a kiss. I had to walk outside and check the sky for flying pigs. The baby slept through all of their lessons. No one threw a tantrum at the table. Small wins, man, small wins. All I could do was thank God for crockpots and completed to-do lists. I rocked today; I was Pinterest worthy. I should have posted a picture of the kids working quietly on Facebook so the world could see what a great domestic engineer I am. Hell, I even got the bathrooms clean. I prefer to be paid in wine and

Books-A-Million gift cards. If only someone could pass that memo to my husband, who insists on paying me in penis.

Speaking of whom, guess who still hasn't fixed the ceiling fan or the light in the baby's room. You got it, that guy! He has been home all day too. I told him last night that I really needed that light fixed. I should have known "She doesn't even sleep in there" followed by "Fine, I'll do it in the morning" really equaled "I'm not doing it at all." Fast-forward to around 3 p.m., Kid Three says, "What is that smell?" Kids One and Two point at the baby. I lean in to check her diaper and *voila*! There is poop up her back. I do the whole "I really don't want your poop on me," under-the-arm hold and run all the way to her room so I could clean her up on the changing table and avoid my freshly washed comforter. I flipped the light switch with my elbow, said light flickered, the fan started doing that "I sound like I'm about to fall out of the ceiling" thing, then it fell out of the fucking ceiling. It scared me so bad, I forgot why I was in the room in the first place. I grabbed the little poop bomb, cradled her right on out of there, and plopped down next to her on my bed. I was so mad at the husband, I forgot she was a walking Huggies baby wipe commercial until she crawled on my chest. Throw the whole husband away, right along with the baby and what used to be my favorite shirt. As bad as all of that was, I still made it problem-free through my entire day with the rest of the gang, so I won't complain too much more. I'm also not going to Home Depot to buy another ceiling fan. He is on his own with that one.

Dear Diary,

There is nothing more comforting than the smell of a fresh direct deposit. The joy of checking off that first bill or two is almost incomparable. Be it as it may a fleeting joy, but a joy nonetheless. Unfortunately, it is quickly followed by the stomach-turning agony of which bill doesn't get paid so we can have gas, groceries, and diapers for the week.

At this point, I have a love/hate relationship with bill extensions. I'm so sick of this. I get to gray over our budget worries while Mr. Brings Home the Bacon gets to watch YouTube videos about fishing when he's supposed to be figuring out how to install the electrical wires in a ceiling fan. YouTube for husbands equals self-induced ignorant bliss. How is it even possible to love and dislike one person so much? Crying kid approaches...

Dear Diary,

Fun fact: I am not speaking to my husband. Not in a silent-as-a-monk kind of way, but in the "I can't actually *not* speak to you ever because kids are watching" kind of way. I don't know if he's too scared to ask what's wrong or just too stupid to figure it out, but I do know that he purposely tries to strike up conversations while the kids are around. I, however, have mastered the art of the clipped, monosyllabic response. He has until his next payday to fix that fan or I'm going to call one of those hire-a-husband places and pay someone else to do it. That is sure to put his panties in a bunch.

The sad part is he wouldn't even be upset about the fact that we can't afford it; he'd just be bothered that I called someone else to do a job he's claimed multiple times he was going to do. It is amazing how men pull off that whole "how dare you be annoyed

at my total disregard for all the husbandly duties that don't include sex?" thing. It's like they don't even know they're wrong. If I pay someone else to do it, he'll feel all annoyed and self-righteous, but his rebound time is like six seconds. That is almost not even worth the trouble. On top of that, I'm the one who will have to deal with the budget problem I created by paying someone to do something my husband should have fixed before it even broke. He let a fifteen-minute fix turn into a two-hundred-dollar problem. That should really be grounds for divorce.

Dear Diary,

I pinned a list of books for people having a quarter-life crisis the other day, and I realized I already had one of the books on my shelf. And since my budget is getting tighter than my yoga pants, it only made sense to read that one first: *A Lesson Before Dying*. The title just sounded so enlightening. I thought, *Surely, Ernest Gaines has figured something I need to know out.* Interesting book to say the least. Or the most? I enjoyed it, but I was secretly expecting it to give me the answers to *my* quarter-life crisis. It did not. Truthfully, I don't even think the main character got the answers he was looking for.

If variety is the spice of life, then stagnation must be the death of it. If that's true, then my entire life, at this point, is a lesson before dying. Death by budgeting. Death by living paycheck to paycheck. Death by weight gain. Death by stabbing myself in the eye

the very next time I hear the word "mama." Death by slowly being poisoned by the cheap household cleaning products I must use now. Death by stepping on a thousand LEGOs. Death by exhaustion. I'm pretty sure I need therapy. Or Prozac. Or both.

Dear Diary,

You know what's better than wine, chocolate, books, and kid-free days? Winning!

Petty wife moment: I realized I was not willing to waste money on a repairman or an electrician. I may be "haven't had a meaningful conversation with my husband in days" crazy, but I'm not "cut off my own nose to spite my face" crazy. I needed a resolution that brought me to the desired end without stressing me and my poor lil' budget *all* the way out.

Enter stage left, Malika and one strategically placed phone call. As soon as Eric pulled into the driveway, I called Malika. He walked through the door right as I was telling her that the fan in Kizzy's room had fallen out of the ceiling and asking if her husband (nice guy but weird in a "doesn't watch football or drink beer" kind of way—Eric's words,

not mine), the electrician, could help me install a new one.

"Oh no, it's no rush, hun. I'm not even buying a new one until Friday. Thank you so much! Bring the kids when y'all come. I'll make lunch, and we can make a playdate of it. OK, girl, Eric just walked in from work. Let me go. Bye!"

Cherry on the pie, I hung up and started talking to him like I haven't been ice queening him for days. The look on his face was somewhere between rage he won't express and relief at my use of multisyllabic words. Technically, I haven't won yet, but I'd bet my last dollar that he has that fan replaced and running before the week is out. If I stop and think about it, I win either way. If he doesn't fix it, which he definitely will, I'll still get my fan fixed for cheap (because I re-fuse to not pay Dre, no matter what Malika says), and the kids get a fun day with their friends from church that doesn't require anything more than the toys they already have. That's saving money two ways!

Dear Diary,

Rest in peace, my dearly departed dishwasher. You served me well and without complaint for many years. You will be sorely missed. On the upside, my good ole hubby finally fixed the fan. On the downside, if one more thing in this house breaks, I am going to lose it. I strongly considered burning it down today, but I'm pretty sure God wouldn't approve, and I'd end up in jail. I've seen *Orange Is the New Black,* and I am positive that jail is not a good look for me. Normally, I'd say, "Two steps forward, one step back. . ." Wait, I don't think that's right. Hell, it really doesn't even matter at this point because it's no steps forward for us. We are living in a perpetual state of steps backward.

Sometimes I feel like it's my fault. Maybe if I worked, things wouldn't be so hard. We made the decision to homeschool after much prayer and

decided that come hell or high water, we wouldn't give up. I love being home with my kids, but I hate feeling helpless in situations like this. My husband being completely against me finding a job doesn't help either. We've sat down and worked the pros and cons of me going back to work.

Pros:

- ❖ I get out of the house.
- ❖ I bring in extra cash.
- ❖ Nobody at work will call me Mama.

Cons:

- ❖ Procuring and paying for childcare for four children
- ❖ Need an extra vehicle
- ❖ Gas and insurance for extra vehicle
- ❖ Need to purchase clothes that do not include spandex as a major component

Being out of the workforce for so long means I am starting out at entry level, no matter where I go. Eight to eleven dollars an hour isn't even enough to clear out the expenses on the cons list. If I get a job in fast food, I won't need clothes (thank God for uniforms), but that would barely cover my newly incurred child-care expenses. Logically, I realize going back to work won't help while simultaneously adding more stress. Emotionally, I still feel like it's at least doing something. There are only so many coupons I can clip. I just don't know anymore.

Dear Diary,

I figured out my problem. Today, my Happy Planner sticker pack had a shiny, gold sticker that said, "Your vibe attracts your tribe," and I thought, *Clearly, I need a new vibe.* That thought led me to Target because, let's face it, if you can buy a new vibe, Tar-jay is the place you'd want to buy it from. I ended up having my first meaningful conversation of the day with a lady in the yoga aisle. She saw me looking at the meditation and beginner yoga DVDs on the end-cap next to the yoga blocks and twenty-dollar water bottles and asked if I was looking for something in particular.

I'm not sure what in the word vomit happened, but by the time I finished talking, she was telling me that I needed to try burning certain herbs to "cleanse my atmosphere." I wasn't sure whether to slowly back away or ask more questions. I opted to smile

and nod. Burning little bundles of sage throughout my entire house is a little too "hippy," if not a little too witchcraft-y, for me.

Minus weird rituals, possible witchcraft, and illicit drug use, how does one actually go about changing their vibe? Target doesn't sell new vibes or sage. I should just ditch the tribe. That might be easier.

Dear Diary,

I thank God for days like today. The hubs was off of work. It stormed all day, which wasn't a problem because there was nowhere to go anyway. We just stayed inside and did nothing. I cooked a light breakfast and lunch, then we had leftovers for dinner. We watched movies all day, so the house stayed clean. It was just a peaceful, easy day.

Of course, it was sprinkled with the usual kid drama but nothing crazy or unexpected for a gang of young boys. The biggest arguments we had to diffuse were about what we were going to watch next. I could use two days like this every week.

Dear Diary,

So, I did a thing. I created a self-care board on Pinterest last night and pinned a bunch of blog posts and infographics that will allegedly help me reclaim my life. I was watching *Alice in Wonderland* with the kids and realized that I have, in fact, lost my muchness. I used to be so much-y, but now . . . not so much.

Is being a wife and mom at the cost of yourself worth it? The more I think about it, the more I realize that I don't even know who I am anymore. When did mom buns and stretch pants become signature parts of my life? If I put on jeans, when I can find a pair in the closet that fits, all of my kids trail me through the house asking me where I'm going. They act like they've seen a ghost when I put on lipstick and a dress. My life has become an endless loop of workout pants I don't work out in, too-big T-shirts,

and old-lady church clothes, a.k.a a possibly cute blouse a seventy-five-year-old grandma would wear with rotating black slacks and ballerina flats.

My nineteen-year-old self would be so disappointed if she, with all her dreams about her future fabulousness, saw me today. When did I stop buying CDs and listening to all the different kinds of music I love? Clearly, it was a long time ago because I don't even think people buy CDs anymore. When did I decide that wearing T-shirts that are two sizes too big all the time was an acceptable way to live? Your thirties should be the time of your life. Mine has turned out to be an endless rotation of laundry left in the washer too long and learning videos on YouTube. Hopefully finding myself is as easy as singing a few songs and going on a boat trip. Why not? Hell, it worked for Moana. I'm off to price cruises.

Dear Diary,

I hate parents who don't know how to keep their sick kids at home. No set of plans are so important that you cannot cancel. If you or your child has the sniffles, stay home. If you or your child has a fever, stay home. If you or your child has thrown up for an unknown reason in the last twenty-four hours, *stay home*. I know Jesus frowns on throat punches. I know He does. But God, did I want to throat punch somebody's mama today!

The kids had a playdate today. A few of the stay-at-home moms at my church decided, in an effort to stave off our impending burnouts, we would rotate keeping each other's children for three hours while the other moms went and did whatever. Take a nap, mop without screaming, "Get out of here!" every five minutes, see a movie, read a book, whatever. Just free time. It started off with a group of five of us. We pulled numbers to figure out the initial schedule,

then we would just keep rotating months until other moms joined.

Month one was fine. Malika hosted, and I saw a movie by myself. I did it up too. Popcorn, soda, and a box of Raisinets. The life, I tell you, *the life*! Month two, Sarah hosted, and one of her kids hit one of Malika's kids in the eye with a truck, and there was a whole stink about it. Malika quit after that. Month three, Janice, who participated in the first two months, cancelled when it was her turn to host. Alleged family emergency. Well, lucky number four, my turn to host, and everyone (minus Malika but including Janice) dropped off their kids, and all is well with the world until mid-*The Very Hungry Caterpillar* craft when Katelyn throws up right onto her pile of colored cotton balls. You know what's worse than your own kids' throw up? Other peoples' kids' throw up.

Horrible person alert: I had the strong urge to set her outside on the porch and call her mother. After a few seconds, the urge passed, and I cleaned her up, threw her in some boy clothes, and called her mom. At first, I thought it was something I fed her, then this happened.

Me: Is Katelyn allergic to fish or anything?

Janice: No, why?

Me: She just threw up all over the craft table.

Janice: OMG (she actually said O-M-G), is she OK?

Me: She still looks a little peakish, but I cleaned her up. She is sipping a ginger ale right now. I thought it was the tuna.

Janice: Oh no, she wasn't feeling well and threw up last night. I thought she was fine when she hadn't thrown up again this morning. She must have a little stomach virus or something.

Me: . . . *thinking many un-Christ-like things that I can't say out loud*

Janice: I will be there in a bit to pick her up.

Me: OK?

Janice did not come back for that child until the regular pickup time. Sarah panicked when I told her. Apparently, her and Jake are leaving for vacation soon, and she doesn't want sick babies. Understandable. Janice seemed very nonchalant and falsely apologetic about her willingness to risk infecting all of our kids so she wouldn't miss her three hours of free time. When I mentioned the chances of the other kids getting sick, she hightailed it out of there with Patient Zero and a bag full of vomit-covered clothes. I think I should get an extra crown in Heaven for resisting the urge to trip her on the way out. How selfish can you be? I would have never. I'm pissed, like, beyond pissed!

Dear Diary,

I hate my kids. Well, not all of them. But that damn six-year-old, boy, I tell ya! Him, I could do without. Today, I told all the kids to draw a family portrait during class time, and Kid Two's picture looked like this

I have never wanted to fight a kid so badly in my life. Unfortunately, fighting kids, even your own kids, is frowned upon in most societies. So instead, I hid in my room and ate candy out of their treasure box.

Sidenote: The treasure box needs fresh candy.

Dear Diary,

You should know that any day that starts with poop on the stairs will not end well. It is damn near impossible to clean diarrhea out of the grooves in wooden bunk bed steps. As I sat there, scrubbing the step grooves with a dingy toothbrush, I realized this is rock bottom. Whatever dreams I had have died, and I am stuck in the purgatory that is parenthood. The sheer volume of vomit multiple kids can upchuck is as astounding as it is disgusting. I just want to move into the shower and stay there. Everyone will be fine within the next twenty-four to thirty-six hours, which is probably right around the time I'll start feeling sick.

Apple cider vinegar and raw honey shots all around followed by some good ole probiotics. I have a love/hate relationship with ACV, but you really can't tell based on how much I use it. Everyone

will be fine within the next day-and-a-half, and I'm going to say it until I believe it. I just have to make it through the rest of today. I just have to make it through today.

Upside: Sick kids sleep a lot. I got all the vomit out of the carpet, all the poop off of the stairs, and I've got buckets by all the beds. Hopefully, the hard part is over. My husband thinks I'm lucky because I get to stay home, but sometimes I think he's lucky for getting to leave. I really need to shower and wash my hair. I can't promise that I won't attack Janice like a wild cat the next time I see her.

Dear Diary,

According to Pinterest, I should care for myself today by waking a few minutes early to journal about what I'm grateful for. You know, start the day off on a positive note.

- ❖ I am grateful for having a husband who loves me and expresses it in word and deed.
- ❖ I am grateful for my children being healthy, smart, and beautiful.
- ❖ I am grateful for being able to stay home and care for my family the way I want to.
- ❖ I am grateful that I have a roof over my head (even though I could only afford to pay half of the mortgage last month).
- ❖ I am grateful I have food to eat.
- ❖ I am grateful I am alive.

No matter how today turns out, I can always be thankful for those things.

That is my Pinterest-approved list. I should post it on Facebook. It's cute, but a completely honest list would sound more like: "I am grateful for caffeine, drive-throughs, wine, cartoons, DoorDash, naps, books, wine, caffeine, Olive Garden, books, wine, kids, caffeine, husband, wine, life, books, steak-houses, Amazon Prime, and wine."

Writing that literally made me laugh out loud. Fun fact: Every time I've ever texted someone, "LOL," I was lying. I never laugh. It's just a politer way to end a text conversation than saying, "Please stop texting me now." "LOL" is my newspeak for "conversation over." Dear God, I just wrote "newspeak."

Note to Self: Do not read *1984* not a n'an 'nother time.

Dear Diary,

Today, I started a new read aloud with the kids, and I think I've figured out what's happening in my life. If life really does imitate art, then clearly, one of the little goblins from *The Spiderwick Chronicles* is living in my house. I'm willing to bet that if I tore a hole in the kitchen wall, I'd find a gross little nest made comfy with all of the kid-sized socks that have gone missing. Keeping a family of six socked is expensive. My socks last forever. There is no earthly explanation for how many of my children's socks don't have matches. I was doing their laundry today, and if I matched three pairs of socks from a week's worth of laundry for three kids, that was a lot. Goblins in the wall are the only rational explanation at this point.

I'm <----------> this close to buying everyone flip-flops and just eliminating the need for socks altogether. Is it bad parenting to tell your children

how stressed out you are about the fact that it costs twenty-one dollars to buy three new packs of socks? A quick economics lesson would do them some good. I should make up a class called Household Economics where they learn about how much socks, toilet paper, paper towels, liquid soap, and natural cleaning products cost. I could make a pie chart showing what percentage of our household income is spent on these items then give them assignments where they have to figure out how to use less of those things or use them more efficiently.

I wonder if that's too much for four kids, all nine and under. I'm going to post it in that homeschool group on Facebook and see what they think. I'm quite sure at least one other person in that group does that already.

Dear Diary,

For a second, I thought I had eyeballed our budget so I would be prepared for payday ahead of time. Everything was OK-ish on paper until I realized I forgot to budget a kid's birthday (facepalm). Talk about a parenting fail. Between the sick kids, the financial stress, and my general, all-around, Eeyore-level mopiness, Kid Two's birthday completely slipped my mind. Now I have to figure out when that guy I married is off so we can actually do something for said kid's birthday, seeing as dads are important at these kinds of things. Once I figure out when we can do "It," then I have to figure out what "It" is, only to be upstaged by how I am going to pay for "It."

Gifts. Crap, I still forgot gifts. I know he wants a tablet, and I almost feel obligated to make it happen because he already has middle child syndrome, and this will be the perfect chance for him to get a cool

thing first. Fiscally irresponsible, yes. But it will do loads for his self-esteem. Now that I've written that, I feel like that is probably horrible parenting. I can feel the spirit of one thousand perfect moms telling me I should teach him that his worth comes from God and not his material belongings. And you know what, Spirit Susan? You could be right, but a) the majority of adults struggle with that concept, so how well do you really expect my six-year-old with middle child issues to take it, and b) who doesn't want to one-up their older brother at least once?

Solution: I'll tell him all the things and still get him the tablet for his birthday. Now back to paying for it. *I* don't even own a tablet. Is it even a reasonable gift for a six-year-old? Probably not. Good thing he's making seven.

Dear God,

Make me a bird so I can fly far, far, far away from here. Dear God, make me a bird so I can fly far, far, far away from here.

Now I want to watch *Forrest Gump*.

Dear Diary,

Sometimes I pick up this pen, and I don't even know where to start. I'm tired of complaining. Complaining or venting? Either way, I'm tired of it. But I also don't feel like being positive all the time. I'm like the great freaking pretender. I'm all smiles and "It's fine," but inside, I feel like I'm falling apart. Who can you tell that you feel like your life has hit a standstill? Who wants to admit that sometimes they cry in the shower so their husband won't see and ask, "Why are you crying?" which will only send them into a further tailspin because the honest answer is "I don't know"? Who can you tell, judgement- and "I told you so"- free, that sometimes you wish you'd sent your kids to school because you can't take a. single. 'nother. tantrum. at the table?

One of my children says, "Excuse me, ma'am," so much that I cringe when people say it to me in public.

I hide in the bathroom in the middle of the day, and I love books so much because none of them call me Mom or offer unsolicited advice about my choice to home educate. I feel like a well-put-together mess. My Sunday game face is a sad farce, and I'm tired of putting it on. I feel stuck, like I'm walking in muck and getting nowhere, but I'm still exhausted from all the walking.

I want to be, do, and experience so much, but I don't feel very much-y right now. The Mad Hatter summed up my life in a single line, and now it's stuck in my head. I have lost my muchness, and there's nothing worse than feeling like you are not very much.

Dear Diary,

This self-care challenge from Pinterest is not going so well. Today, I was supposed to doll myself up and do my makeup—and not for my husband or anyone else—just because I am beautiful and worth it. The problem is I don't know how to put on makeup. Bigger problem: I'm a classic overachiever. I spent at least two hours watching makeup tutorials on YouTube, then I wasted thirty dollars going out and buying all the stuff the videos claimed I needed to achieve a "look." What did I learn today? That YouTube and the devil are both liars.

My first look (I was going for jazzy) can only be described as "clown face," and I kid you not, the clown wore it better. My second look screamed, "Someone put this on me after I died!"

New self-care lesson for the day: Mascara and lipstick are enough.

Dear Diary,

I am pretty sure I should start having sex with my husband before he starts having sex with someone else. I feel like it's inevitable. I'm pretty sure if he ever did cheat, it would feel like the most devastating thing that ever happened to me, but somehow, that still doesn't motivate me to initiate sex. I'm not sure if my lack of drive is postpartum, regular ole depression, hormones from the birth control, or my general disgust with my body right now. I know Eric thinks my low sex drive has something to do with him. He has gently implied it, but he's too passive aggressive to outright say it. Ugh, men and their secret hyper-sensitive thoughts.

I really don't know what to do. If I get back on antidepressants, that will just lower my drive more, like last time. If I get off birth control, I'll get pregnant again during the temporary boost, only to lose it again

to the depression from being pregnant, broke, and getting fatter *again.* This feels like a lose-lose situation to me. I'm too young for these kinds of problems. Somewhere in the world, there is a sixty-two-year-old woman going to town with her Viagra-filled husband, and I'm just here . . . journaling.

- ❖ Knowing you need to do better + Having no desire to do better = Doing nothing
- ❖ Sexless husband + Uninterested wife = Porn and masturbation

*Outcome highly probable

I've always been good with math. Who would've known I'd use it after college?

Dear Diary,

I had a need, and God met it! And to top it all off, I didn't even have to order any miracle spring water to get it (insert praise dance here).

There wasn't a $100,000 check in the mail, but my baby will get his tablet now. Well, now that I've written that, I realize it was more of a want than a need. But then again, I think the desire to give your children what they want feels a lot like a need from the parental side of things. I *need* to make them happy. Sometimes the desire to not disappoint little people who are probably going to put you in a nursing home one day is overwhelming.

Anywho, I was on the phone with my parentals this morning, and per their standard, Mom had me on speakerphone, and Dad was randomly chiming in from his workbench. (Sidenote: It is still super gross how clingy they are. Like how much time should they

actually spend together? It's weird, but I digress.) So, I'm giving Lil her bi-weekly breakdown of my life. The usual. Who pooped on what. Who passed a benchmark that proves she doesn't have to call DCF on me for educational neglect . . . just yet. And my daddy, God bless him, says "Lil, isn't Chris's birthday coming up soon?" The fact that he asked her like I wasn't right there on speakerphone was a smidge annoying, but again, I digress.

After my mom told him it was in a few days, that dad of mine said, "Right, what'd we send him?" And instead of answering him, my mom launched right into an inquiry of what Chris wants and if it was Amazon Prime-able. When I mentioned my hesitation to buy him a tablet because of his age and the price, I was immediately outvoted by two old people who apparently have very little respect for the budget they live on.

All I had to do was send her a link to the one I wanted for him, and bam, two days from now, I'll have a shiny new tablet to wrap for him with an adorable little Amazon gift note that says, "Happy Birthday, Christian! Love Papaw James and Mamaw Lillian." When she sent me the screenshot of the confirmation, I thought two things: 1) *Thank you, Jesus*, and 2) *Who taught Mama how to screenshot?*

I ordered him a case in his favorite color, and I'm going to get him an iTunes card because, according to Google, that is the best way for him to pay for games online. It's a win-win for me. I wonder if they would have ordered one for me too if I had bought some of that miracle spring water?

Dear Diary,

I have been on a quest to find out where exactly I lost my muchness. In true Wonderland fashion, this quest has led me down a series of random yet interconnected rabbit holes. I did figure out that I never actually stopped loving music, though; I just stopped listening to it. I used to listen to everything: country, rap, oldies, neo-soul, alternative, R&B, and not-so-heavy metal/rock. If someone would have shuffled through the CDs in my car, they would have had no idea what color I was. I listened to everything. But then, my oldest hit the mimicking stage and off went the radio. Your two-year-old quoting a full Lil Wayne bar in church is bound to cause a knee-jerk reaction. Let's just say I clutched my own pearls. Then, I got *"saved*, saved,"* and the church said worldly music was a heinous sin, so off the radio stayed. Then,

when I finally tried to turn it back on, I could not understand what anyone was saying.

Radio: Anta, anta, anta, anta, anta, anta

Me: Why is his panda in Atlanta? He really shouldn't be giving bears Fanta; that can't be good for them.

Husband: He's talking about a car.

Me: Why is his car in the Atlanta Zoo?

Husband: *facepalm*

Me: *turns radio back off*

Now my life consists of songs you can sing in church and a random shuffle of songs from *Moana, Trolls*, and *Sing*. I'm not sure what the middle ground is, but as a start, I paid for (gasp) Apple Music today so me and Adele can have a good ole time mopping these floors. Hopefully, I'll be telling this much less much-y version of myself "Hello from the other side" soon.

Dear Diary,

Sometimes I feel like the best thing I ever did was make all these babies and stay home to love, nurture, and educate them. Other times, I want to shoot myself in the face (or at least in the foot). Can you guess which time I had today? I bet you guessed right! (Of course, you guessed right, fool; you're talking to yourself.)

We're all mad here!

Dear Diary,

I hate cats. There was a hungry, crying little stray around our house yesterday, and I caught the boys feeding it. It's still here, and I have the looming feeling that it is soon going to be a pet. How can you argue with huge, glistening puppy dog eyes and "But Mommy, God would want us to help anyone in need. He made the kitty too."?

Religion Class Question #1: Who made you?
Answer: God

Religion Class Question #2: What else did he make?
Answer: Everything

I never saw that lesson coming back to bite me in my sizable rear. I'm not sure if this is a homeschool win or blatant manipulation. I should have told them that God made me too, and he probably didn't like

you drawing that fat mama picture, but it would be just my luck that this would have been the day God started back smiting people for using his name in flip comments to small people and being mean to animals. I can't win. I should let the little crumb snatchers watch *Constantine* so they can see what cats are really about, but I'm sure that's bad parenting.

Well, I'm off to go clean the kitchen, which I've been avoiding all day.

Dear Diary,

I need a quick and easy party idea. I tried pinning party ideas but quit as soon as I realized that I don't have the time. And I don't even mean that in a "I have too much to do" kind of way either. I mean it in a "Sweet Brown's 'Ain't nobody got time for that'" kind of way. I am trying so hard to can, and I cannot. I can't decide between here or there, trucks, dinosaurs, or sports, store-bought décor (expensive) or homemade (time-consuming). I'm just not here for it.

It would be easier if this party was for any kid but Christian, and I do mean any kid. He wields his second-born slight like a weapon of mass destruction that's specially designed to destroy my last damn nerve. Of course, the husband has no opinion on what to do for him, so there's that.

I just don't understand how a kid can be so upset about not being born first or last. I used to think

middle child syndrome was an excuse parents made up for their problem child, but it's very real. Chris seemed like he knew from conception that he was going to be Kid Two for the rest of his life. He even looked mad about it in his ultrasound pictures. If it was any of my other children's birthdays, it wouldn't even matter. Kid One is in that odd "I'm a pre-pre-pre-teen" phase and doesn't care about anything but Fortnite kills and lame YouTube videos. I could grab a box of pizza and tell him three kids of his choice could come play video games with him, and he'd be thoroughly satisfied. Thoroughly. Kids Three and Four are too young to even care. Well, unless I want to add to the growing list of things he's going to tell his therapist about, I better figure something out ASAP. The weekend is fast approaching.

Dear Diary,

Today was the funniest (and the worst) birthday party I've ever thrown. Apparently, you just can't know what you don't know about your kids. So the Bringer Home of the Bacon brought it home, and I burnt it all up by booking a party for fifteen kids at Chuck E. Cheese. In the spirit of being fiscally responsible, I sprung for the cheapest party they had: star package with an extra pizza, check! $261.33 later, I was all set. Well, that plus gifts and a cake to bring with us today.

My children have always loved Chuck E. Cheese. I was sure I'd end today with a World's Best Mom award. Just sure of it. We hadn't been in a while, so we were really surprised at all of the upgrades. They don't even use tokens anymore. Everything was going fine—amazing even. Malika and Dre came with their kids. Sarah showed up solo with her gang because, apparently, James couldn't leave his nine-to-five to

come to a party from 5 p.m. to 7 p.m., but I digress. The neighbor brought her boys. Janice couldn't make it because I accidentally (on purpose) didn't text her the invite until this morning. (Oops.) Just perfect . . . until the curtain pulled back for the band show to start.

Fun fact: Sarah didn't actually watch the kids when it was her turn to, which totally makes Truck-Gate make more sense. Like I said, the lights dimmed, the curtains pulled back, and the animatronic band members started moving and singing. Two out of four of my kids and one of Malika's kids *lost* it. I mean, they went batshit crazy. Malika had to drag Mikey kicking and screaming from beneath the table he dove under. My nine-year-old started screaming, "Run, they're coming," because he's a mini asshole who is not being raised right. The birthday boy, in all of his newfound seven-year-old glory, ran over his four-year-old brother and gave him a nasty rug burn while he was trying to hightail it out of there. And I'm just standing there like an idiot, wearing a baby, gen-uinely confused, and trying really hard not to laugh.

Let's just say the party was over after that. After much prodding on the ride home, we learned that Sarah's version of babysitting was letting the kids watch YouTube videos. She is not as strict concerning some of the things her kids watch so all of our children ended up watching what sounds like an hour's worth of *Five Nights at Freddy's* videos. I'm not sure if it's a game, a movie, or a show, but whatever it is, you have to survive various killer animatronics or something like that, which explains why they've been refusing to sleep without the closet light on for the past two months. This entire day turned out to be a giant waste of a bill extension.

We ended up eating cake and opening the gifts at home alone after we left. And as some form of instant karma for laughing at a group of terrified four- to seven-year-olds, when I asked Christian how I could make him feel better after the animatronic attack ruined his birthday, he said let them keep the kitten.

They named him (or her) Cat.

Dear Diary,

Malika called today, and I made the mistake of telling her what the kids told me about *Five Nights at Freddy's*. YouTube-Gate brought up her still hard feelings about Truck-Gate, which segued into the recent horror Vomit-Gate had been. All in all, I've decided that I won't be participating in the stay-at-home mom support group anymore. I really do need a new tribe.

Dear Diary,

I am convinced that babies have a "mommy is do-ing something" radar that jolts them awake halfway through any attempted task. I don't think I'll ever be able to mop again. I've been on page twenty-eight of *Metamorphoses* for an entire week now, and quite frankly, I'm impressed that I made it that far.

If I don't start reading more and talking to people less, I'm going to have a nervous breakdown. I need a people-free day.

Possible Solutions:

* Read while holding the baby
* Put phone on airplane mode
* Start back mopping when the kids move out

Bam! Problems solved. See how easy that was?

Dear Diary,

I have to do something to spice up my marriage. Or maybe I need to do a combination of things? If I could stress less about money, we could date without me having to feel like a trip to Saltgrass is going to bankrupt us. And if I lost some freaking weight, maybe I'd feel more like a sexpot instead of Mrs. Potts. Whatever is to blame, I have to do something. I'm pretty sure we are one more conversation about baby poop and boy farts away from being content, co-parenting roommates. If you can even call me doing all the things and him working co-parenting.

The worst part is my desire to spice things up is purely obligatory. Saying it's more for him than for me is a vast understatement. In my defense, it's kind of hard to want to sleep with a guy who you have to explain that "to find something, you have to actually move stuff around and not just stand in the room

with your hands on your hips glancing from side to side" at least twice a week. Maybe that's the real problem. Maybe I'm not too fat or depressed for sex. Maybe I'm just not a pedophile and, therefore, not attracted to children, no matter how tall they are.

Dear Diary,

Life is a daring adventure or nothing at all.

Clearly, I'm stuck in the "nothing at all" part right now. You know what? I take that back. Maybe chasing these children is all the adventure I need. Besides, my budget called today and said that's all the adventuring I can afford right now anyway. I guess I should try to make the most of it and enjoy it.

I saw a post online about vaccine-related deaths and injuries today that brought me to tears. There were so many pictures and videos of children before and after their shots. It was terrifying. Some of those posts just ripped my heart out. The worst part was the mothers in the comments were tearing each other apart. I get disagreeing about something, but these women were going back and forth calling each other stupid, saying people's kids should be taken from them. The worst of it were the moms—*mothers,* for

crying out loud—mothers who not only thought it because, let's face it, thinking this is horrible enough, but posted out in the open on a public thread for God and everyone to read that they wished each other's children would die.

Any argument that leads to adults wishing disease, disorder, and death on children is one that should not be had. Ever. One side was hoping kids died of scarlet fever and the pox as a sign that their stupid-ass mothers should have had them vaccinated. The other side was wishing autism and SIDs on children and babies, also as a sign that their stupid-ass mothers should not have vaccinated them. There were a thousand links, and each one I clicked said the exact opposite of the one I had read before. Then, I ended up in some rabbit hole about dead doctors— well, murdered doctors. It was all too much.

I've never felt bad or afraid about my kids getting their shots. It's just what we do. Pre-homeschooling groups on Facebook, I didn't even know this was a thing people fought over, let alone fought to draw blood over. I've never been so appalled and confused in my life. My kids are vaccinated. Why would I be upset with another mother because her kids aren't? If my kids have had their shots, I don't have to be afraid of Susan's unvaccinated kids getting the measles because mine *have had their shots*! I don't get what I'm missing here. And even if Susan's kid gets the measles then gives said measles to my kid (which I don't think can happen because they've had their shots), it's OK; it's the freaking measles, not the bubonic plague. I am really tempted to leave all these online mom groups. The kicker is these are private mom groups solely for the purpose of moms seeking support and information (be it about schooling, potty training, or breastfeeding). I'd bet my last two dollars that every mom in those groups, no matter what side of an issue they fall on, want the absolute best for their kids. How did something that was meant to be supportive turn into moms wishing dead babies on each other? We need a new Noah-level flood. I'll never understand how anyone could be that cruel to a mother who's mourning the loss of her child. Never.

Well, that turned into quite the rant. Lack of adventure or not, I have a lot to be grateful for. After today, my next adventure is going to be vaccine research. It seems like the kind of research that necessitates copious amounts of wine.

Dear Diary,

I am a rock star! I had a baby. I literally made him from scratch and then grew him in my body. I pushed him into this world through insurmountable pain, fed him from my breasts, and grew him into a strong, healthy kid. And today, this day, I can finally say I have taught him to read! I am Queen of the Homeschoolers.

Dear Diary,

I pinned a bunch of stuff to my marital improvement board in the spirit of not becoming soon-to-be-divorced, empty nesters eighteen years from now. I decided to actively try and spice things back up, and I've never been so stressed out in my life. I pinned a seven-day sex challenge, and I realized I may be too old and married for this. Where does one have sex outside when you're thirty-plus with four kids? What public restroom do you have sex in, and who watches the kids for all these sexcapades? A public restroom? Seriously? That sounds like an infectious disease waiting to happen.

With the advent of camera phones and social media, nowhere is safe. Everyone is just one wrong move from being a Facebook clip. Having gross public bathroom sex tops the list of things you do not want your kids to stumble upon on Google. The

thought alone is enough to confine all sexual activity to the privacy of your home.

The closest one to doable is day five, which said to try a new place in your house. Problem: What is more of a turnoff than a healthy and not-so-irrational fear of your nine-year-old catching you having sex in the kitchen during the wee hours of the morning? I make baby food on those counters, for crying out loud! This is going to be harder than I thought.

We are not even going to talk about how I've gained way too much weight to be trying new positions. All the suggestions the pin gave just made me want to go to the gym. I guess he'll have to be happy with seven days of hiding in the closet so the baby can't see or hear us have sex.

Sidenote: She needs to move into her own room.

Dear Diary,

It is my favorite time of the year. I put up my fall decorations on August 1 every year, willing fall to come earlier and earlier. It rarely works though. The leaves are finally beginning to change, the weather is cooling off (not enough to know if we'll get a real winter this year, but enough), my kids will soon be fall tree and pumpkin crafted to death, and all the bugs are preparing to go back to hell where they came from.

The only downside to pumpkin spice season is that my favorite online forums are this <---> close to starting their yearly arguments about who celebrates what or not and why and what because blah, blah, blah. There is nothing more unappealing than two Christians beating each other to death about what and how to celebrate. Correction: Even this is not as unappealing as the Mommy Vaccine Wars, but it is a shoe in for spot number two on my list of Things That

Do Not Appeal to Me Whatsoever. But anywho, last September, I posted a cute picture of my kids painting pumpkins to decorate our porch for fall, and a lady in my Christian homeschool group told me I was encouraging my children to participate in devil worship. She was only outdone by the one in December who told me gingerbread men come from pagan yule celebrations and are symbolic of ritualistic cannibalism. I mean, come on, Susan; it's just freaking cookies.

Sometimes I wish I could stand up in the middle of the room, or thread—whatever—and scream, "Shut up! We don't care!" Does whoever posting pictures of her keeping the Christ in Christmas by baking Jesus a birthday cake with her kids have to start the "You know it's not even his birthday" fight every year? We know! I just want to say, "Simmer down, ladies. Some of us are just here for spelling curricula suggestions." I'm over it already, and it hasn't even started yet. Solution: Log off of Facebook.

Dear Diary,

Clearly, I took too much credit the other day, and God did not like it. Today, my newest addition to the Kids Mommy Taught How to Read Club couldn't read a lick. It took us forty-five minutes to get through one reader. I'm pretty sure that was the shortest-lived victory in the history of victories.

My life's recent win stats:

* Me: 1
* Kid: 674
* God: 47,385

Dear Diary,

I can't shake the feeling that I am failing at everything all the time. I have lists on top of lists of what I need to change, but nothing is changing. I've done nothing. Every area of my life is out of order.

- ❖ My finances are jacked.
- ❖ I'm discouraged about my decision to homeschool.
- ❖ My marriage is awfully close to becoming passionless, a.k.a over.
- ❖ I don't feel edified at church anymore, but I'm not sure how to leave without people thinking I'm a butt-naked sinner. The bigger issue is that I care what people think at all.
- ❖ My weight is out of *control.*

I feel lost, which is horrible because I'm holding lists on top of lists full of directions. Sometimes the

distance between knowing and doing is immensely hard to traverse. What is wrong with me? This has to be deeper than plain ole laziness. I think I'm broken. I don't even know where to go for help. I can't afford a real therapist, and if I go to the free counseling at church, they're just going to say I have a demon. Looks like it's just me and you, babe.

Dear Diary,

That is my frustration. If anyone sees this, they are going to think I am nuts. Not "Oh, she's crazy; how cute" nuts either, but "Somebody break out the meds" nuts.

Dear Diary,

God is good. He is faithful. He loves me with a perfect love. Perfect love casts out all fear. God is faithful. He will do all He promised. He can do all He said. I can trust Him because His thoughts toward me are good. I can hope in my future because He will complete the work He has started in me. God is love. He loves me right now as much as He ever has or ever will. His love for me is not based on my performance. He loves me, and He is faithful. He is faithful. He is God alone, and He is faithful. His ways are just and perfect. He sends rain for the just and the unjust. He reigns over the just and the unjust. He is my God, He loves me, and I can trust Him because He is faithful. His strength is made perfect in my weakness, and I can trust that when I am weak, He will strengthen me because He is faithful. God is love, and He loves me right

now, today. Not tomorrow when I pray more or last month because I fasted, but right now, today. He loves me because I am His, and He is love. He is love and is faithful in loving me. The God I serve is a good God. I can trust Him because He is faithful, and He loves me.

Dear Diary,

I feel so bad for my friend. Her mom died unexpectedly, and I have no idea how to comfort her. I was trying to think of practical ways to help her through, but I'm not sure what type of support she needs or doesn't need. I *think* I would prefer to be left alone, but normal people may want friends and family around more in times like this. I don't want to give her the space I would want and make her feel abandoned, but I also don't want to smother her if she just needs time and space to process.

I haven't had enough experience with death to be good at this. God, please give her peace and me the wisdom I need to best support her as she grieves. I absolutely do not want to turn into one of those "I'm sorry for your loss. God needed another angel" grief parrots. Life is ridiculously hard.

Thank God my parents are both alive and healthy.

Dear Diary,

Being socially awkward can be a gift and a curse. Today, it was a gift among gifts. So last night, I texted Jaz and asked her if she wanted me to pass by today. I did not mention dead moms or anything like that because that just doesn't feel like texting material. I legit almost turned around when I got there because there were so many cars in her driveway and up the street. The only thing that stopped me was that I had fried her some chicken, and nobody wants cold chicken. Fried chicken may not be standard grief food, but I figured it would go well with all the casseroles and cakes people were going to bring.

When you think about it, cake seems like too happy of a food to bring over because someone's dead, unless you didn't really like the person. (Note to Self: Bake an angel's food cake in the event of any one of my wretched sister-in-law's untimely demise.)

Anywho, Jaz's husband opened the door and pointed me in her direction. Her pain was palpable. I don't think I've ever felt the way grief looks on her. She looked too sad to cry, and that is a whole 'nother kind of sadness. I thought to myself, *I know it's weird, but I brought you chicken because I don't want you to be too sad that your mama died, and maybe it'll help because I fry really good chicken.* I wanted to say, "How are you holding up?" I was slightly anxious and *really* uncomfortable, so I thought, *How are you holding up?* but said, "I know it's weird, but I brought you chicken because I don't want you to be too sad that your mama died, and maybe it'll help because it's really good chicken."

Jaz's face dropped instantly, which made me panic internally, unleashing a word vomit explaining that I didn't mean she shouldn't be sad because dead moms make people really sad and that's a normal kind of sad, and she could be as sad as she wanted and please just take the chicken because it's only going to get worse if I don't stop talking now. I have never seen Jaz laugh so hard in my life. Then, the entire family looked at me like I had done something horribly inappropriate Because, apparently, you are not allowed to laugh when you have a dead mama, and all I could think to do like a damn fool was hold out the pan and say, "Chicken, anyone?"

It was mortifying, but I made Jaz laugh, so it was worth it. We ended up sneaking off to the backyard to chitchat for a bit before I left. I told her I had no idea how to be her friend or help her through this, and she asked me to fry some more chicken for her mom's repass because it was, in fact, really good chicken. Overall, I think it went well.

Dear Diary,

There is nothing like hot coffee and a slow kid-free stroll through the bookstore. Let us pause there to say, "Thank God for husbands." He probably thinks I'm on the brink of a nervous breakdown, and this was his small way of bringing me back from the edge. Works for me.

I sipped and perused, sipped and perused, then sipped and perused some more. People are looking at me right now like, "What kind of weirdo journals in a bookstore coffeeshop?" but who cares? When I leave here, I am going to eat a Chipotle bowl in the car, and no one is going to call me Mommy or ask for a bite. Then, I am going to walk through Target's dollar spot and buy forty dollars' worth of cute educational stuff that I may or may not ever use. Perfection; it is going to be perfection.

Dear Diary,

I may not speak fluent kid, but I am convinced that "Hey, Mom" is newspeak for "Hey, Doer of the Things, come do things for me." It just *has* to mean that. There is no other explanation. Every time I hear, "Hey, Mom," it is immediately followed by a request to feed something, fix something, clean something, or find some lost thing. I try to do all the things or, at least, some of the things most of the time, but sometimes I'm just tired of being doer of the things. I just want to do nothing. Just once, I want to be in the confines of my home and not be the doer of the things.

"Hey, Dad" is clearly newspeak for "Hey, Dad, where is the doer of the things?" To which his response is always, "She's here or there," or "Honey, this or that kid needs you to do something."

Sometimes I just want to scream, "You can do

the damn things! You are fully capable of doing the things. Just try it, and you will see that it's not even hard things, just things. Just things that need to be done, and you should try to do them because I'm tired of doing the damn things!"

Dear Diary,

Why is it inappropriate to ask a woman her age or weight but perfectly acceptable to openly inquire about her reproductive choices? Strangers think it's perfectly OK to question how many kids you choose to have. Family members think it's just fine to tell you when and when not to have kids. So all of that is fine and cool, but they can't ask Mrs. Elderly So and So how old she is? I swear, sometimes I just want to scream, "Yes, my hands are full, but it's because I'm holding things, not because I have too many children." Pregnant women should really start telling people, "Can I deliver this baby and decide if I like it before I'm required to tell you if I want more or not?" It may not seem like a big deal, but it's super annoying. Why are what should be private family decisions fair game, but I can't ask you how much you make a year?

I'm going to start answering people's "innocent," inappropriate questions by asking my own innocent, inappropriate questions.

"As a woman of a certain age, do you struggle with vaginal dryness?"

"I see those gray hairs, mister. Have you tried Viagra yet?"

"So, how was your last pap smear? HPV-free, I'm sure!"

Dear Diary

Last night, my baby would not sleep *at all*. She was a one-woman show. All I wanted to do was sleep, and all she wanted to do was sing . . . and dance . . . and talk. She da-da-da-da-da-ed with the best of them. At four a.m., we were watching *Little Einsteins* and listening to her daddy snore. She is so freaking cute that I almost didn't mind entering today sleepless. Almost.

I realize I have a love/hate relationship with breastfeeding. I want her to stay my baby forever because she is my last one, but I also cannot wait until she turns one, so I can have my boobs back. The ironic part of all this is that now she's sleeping like an angelic little baby, and I'm so tired that I can't fall asleep.

I heard once, on a podcast I believe, that brain dumping helps clear your mind so you can rest better, but it doesn't really feel like it's working. I'm just

going to go watch *Mickey Mouse Clubhouse* while I fold clothes until I get tired enough to actually sleep when I lie down, which hopefully won't be twenty minutes before Kizzy decides to wake up.

Dear Diary,

So, its payday, and my husband is off. He was just going to let me figure out on my own that they are cutting hours at his job. I asked him if layoffs were on the horizon, and the chipperness of his response tells me he's worried, even though his words said otherwise. I gave him the option of running errands with me or staying home with the kids. I figured at least without the kids I would be able to move around faster. Of course, he opts out of anything that may lead to him ending up in Walmart. Fine with me.

I spent my entire day buying food and household goods, chasing sales, and trying to make the most of all my coupons. Normal errand stuff. I have to fry the chicken for Jaz's mom's repass tomorrow, so I texted her to see how many people they were expecting.

A) Fifty to one hundred people is not a workable estimate.

B) She never said who is paying for this chicken.

I just stood there, staring at my phone, waiting for a Cash App notification or something. Nothing. I guess my agreeing to fry it wrongly conveyed a willingness to pay for it. Stressed me clean out, but I still bought the chicken. You can't really compare financial troubles to dead mommy grief, though. I'll figure the money out later.

And then, as if dead-mama-chicken stress wasn't enough, I get home hours later, and a kid meets me at the door. The first thing out of his mouth was, "Hey, Mom. I'm hungry." I asked my husband if he fed the kids, and his exact response was, "They never told me they were hungry."

I could have beat $100 worth of chicken wings off of him. I can barely articulate the level of rage I felt a) because as an adult and a dad, he should have had enough sense to say, "Hey, it's been a while. Maybe I should feed them." Hell, he could have at least given them a snack. And b) because when have I ever been able to sit in the house for several hours without being constantly hounded for meal after snack after drink after snack after meal?

All I could do was walk back here and shut the door. If he hasn't taken the groceries out of the car or fed those kids by the time I go back up there, I am going to attack him. He is so lucky I refuse to scar my kids by jumping on him like a wild dog. I swear I could just beat him to death with a kitchen towel. The saddest part is if I kill him in a fit of domestic rage, *I'll* go to prison. If I just go back up front to fix the food and tell him how much it bothered me that he didn't do it, I sound like the nagging wife. I can't win.

Dear Diary,

I realized two things today: First, it's weird to go to a funeral for someone you are not emotionally attached to, and second, funerals are just weird in general. I don't understand who thought it was a good idea to sit around a dead body in a room full of real-sad and fake-sad people telling old stories and lies aplenty. It truly is strange. The last thing I want to think about when I'm grieving is ordering programs and planning a party menu. And who made it cool to make shirts with dead people on it? Seriously, who?

I do not want anyone crying into a bowl of red beans and rice over me. I do not want people who wouldn't visit my house visiting a rock to "pay me respect" or wasting money putting flowers I can't see or smell on said rock. Before tonight is over, I'll be Googling funeral traditions to find out where this madness comes from. I should look up other cultures'

practices too. I want to see if Americans are just weird or if the entire world is mad. I guess when you think about it, how people have handled their dead has been weird since Egyptians started mummifying folks.

Dear Diary,

I am one thousand percent sure I am not going in for my Depo shot next week. I think switching to non-hormonal birth control might help with my weight and sex drive. It can't hurt, right? I tried Googling birth control options, but most of the articles just told me how much cancer I would get from one hundred percent of contraceptive methods.

All I know is anything that is too easy to forget will be forgotten, so going back to pills is a no, and if I have to track my cycle or log moon phases, I'll be pregnant before the next full one. I'll figure something out before the Depo really leaves my system though.

Dear Diary,

Last night, I weighed myself, and I'm just going to leave that there because I don't need that kind of negativity in my life. Today, I Googled ways to kick-start weight loss and put together a list of things that may be worth giving a shot. I saw a commercial last night about a weight loss pill I can try free for thirty days. If I don't like the results, I don't have to pay anything but the shipping and processing fee. Hopefully, they'll be in soon, but I'm going to start trying some of this other stuff today.

Drinking more water should be easy; I just need to buy some lemons. I'm going to have to fight my way through those apple cider vinegar shots, but it'll be worth it to burn some of this belly fat. I'll have to look more into intermittent fasting before I pull the trigger on that one. I cannot wait until I no longer look like I ate the cooler, cuter, smaller copy of myself.

Dear Diary,

The funeral and my unfortunate weigh-in really made me take a full step back and reevaluate my life. I went walking yesterday evening and had a moment of clarity. There is just something about kid-free quiet that gets the gears turning. I realized I want my muchness back, but there is more than just my weight holding me back.

How I interact with people plays a big part too. Repass Chicken-Gate made me think about how often I do things to please other people at the cost of my own peace and financial stability. I mean, clearly, friends with dead moms are exempt, but it did make me realize how many times I've gone to a lunch or dinner date I couldn't afford. And how many birthday parties I've gone to with ridiculous gifts because I felt bad about people having to buy

so many gifts for all of my kids' birthdays, only to have the same people never actually buy my kids gifts at all. I need to know which people are adding value to my life and why I am keeping around the ones who don't. I let so many people, things, and expectations drain my time, peace, and energy, and my family and I are clearly getting the short end of the stick.

"Busyness does not equal success."

I need to cut down the things and people in my life. I don't have to hang on to people just because we are family or have a long history. It really is time for me to stop giving grace to everyone around me and not keeping an ounce for myself.

Starting Points:

- ❖ No more commitments.
- ❖ It's OK to say, "No, I can't watch your kids, even if I will just be home with mine."
- ❖ It's OK to say, "I can't take on this ministry assignment or project because I don't feel led to or just have too much going on already."

❖ It's OK to not answer the phone. I am not required to give free counseling to people who rarely ever take good advice anyway.

Oh, yeah. This is a solid plan. I'm about to start practicing my guilt-free "No!" face in the mirror.

Dear Diary,

There is no sound more infuriating than a snoring husband, especially a snoring husband who should be helping. The nerve of him. He was off of work, yet again, and spent the entire day in front of the television. The. Entire. Day. He didn't offer to help clean, he didn't offer to help with breakfast, lunch, or dinner, and he didn't offer to help with school. When I did ask him to at least watch Kizzy, he made so much noise with her that the other kids wouldn't cooperate because they wanted to play too. I'm not a monster, so I let them play and watch TV with him, but now I'm behind on my proposed schooling schedule for the week.

I keep telling myself homeschooling is about freedom, so there's really no reason to be upset about any of those things. Truth is I usually don't really care if we check all the boxes, but there's something triggering

about not being able to check all the boxes when the man I vowed to check all the everythings with forever is present and not aiding in the box-checking or even making the box-checking easier. Then, this man I married walked in our bedroom, saw a mountain of clothes strewn across the bed, and pushed said mountain onto my side of the bed, got under the covers, and went to sleep. The unmitigated gall! He's lying in bed, tucked to his neck, next to a pile of clothes that I know he had to recognize were his own clothes too. I spent a solid five minutes staring at him, just seething. I thought, more seriously than is probably acceptable, about slapping him and pretending like I didn't know what happened when he woke up.

I opted to journal instead. The mature choice? Yes. The gratifying choice? No. You know what? I don't have to take this. I have something for his snoring ass. I'm going to fold just my clothes and put his in a pile on the floor next to his side of the bed. He can step on them in the morning and figure out what to do with them his damn self.

Dear Diary,

I am going to be a rock star domestic engineer to-day (but only in ways that don't directly affect my husband, whose clothes are still on the bedroom floor), then as a reward for rocking, I am going to drink a glass—and by glass, I mean bottle—of wine and catch up on *Grey's Anatomy*. I need to binge-watch the rest of season fourteen so I can watch season fifteen before too many episodes record. #momgoals

Did you seriously just write a # in your journal? You should be ashamed of yourself. OK, writing one hashtag is acceptable, but there are few things more annoying than people ending their Facebook posts with fifteen of them. Does Facebook even do anything with hashtags? It's not like Instagram, right? Folks just out here hashtagging for no reason.

#momgoals #greysanatomy #wine #chillin #net-flixbinge #momlife

#wheniputthekidstobeditsonandpopping #blahblahblahblahblah

Hashtags aside, I do know I'm going to be highly upset if Jackson starts dating Maggie. I really want him and April to reconcile. These love triangles Shonda gives us be too much.

Dear Diary,

I cannot believe Eric's clothes are still on the floor. He hasn't asked why I threw them there, and he has made no attempt to fold or save them. He just rummages through the pile to get what he needs and moves on with his day. He is completely unbothered by it. I, on the other hand, cringe every time I see it. I hate it here.

Dear Diary,

Sometimes I think I'm mean to my husband for reasons I cannot fully articulate. I mean, when I'm *mad* mad, I feel like he fully deserves it. Then, I hear what some of the people I know are going through, and I think maybe, just maybe, I'm a spoiled asshole. Just maybe. It's something to think about. He has such a good attitude about me having a bad one that it makes me feel crazy for being mad. Maybe I am crazy, or maybe it's all a part of his nefarious plan to make me feel guilty about not helping with his laundry.

Dear Diary,

I can't tell if my husband is enjoying all of his new-found time off of work or if it's sending him into a slight depression. He is willingly oblivious about our financial issues, so I think it's more boredom than worry. I mean, either way, how much YouTube can one guy watch? Apparently, the answer is a lot. In an effort to kill several Pinterest boards' worth of activities while simultaneously getting him out of the house, I decided to take the big guy on a date. Fiscally responsible? No. A good opportunity to initiate sex? Absolutely! I got a good date night deal through Groupon, so I saved money booking a room and got a dinner voucher.

I guilt-tripped Frick and Frack into spending the night with the kids so we could go out. Actually, I only asked my mom to babysit, but obviously, she is a package deal, so Dad tagged along too. He said he

was going to take the boys backyard camping, and Mama could stay inside with Kizzy. Last night was probably the most time they have spent apart in the last twenty years. But anyway, Eric only had to work half of the day, so I had the parentals come thirty minutes after he left. I went lingerie shopping and checked into our room at the Holiday Inn Express. I Lysol-ed the bed. I threw rose petals around the floor. I even laid out those fake LED candles. Ambience is important. I went back home and did all the things to be date-ready. I shaved my legs and showered for the first time without a kid busting in the bathroom on me. Thank God for grandparents. I slipped my new undies on under my dress. I fed the baby one last time, and when Eric walked in, I told him to shower and dress quickly because we had reservations.

We didn't, but it sounded cool. I handed him his overnight bag, and we strolled right out the house. Well, after fifteen hugs, nine fist bumps, one hundred questions, seventy-six kisses, and one good cry, we strolled right out the house ready for all the night had in store. We went to Longhorn because a) it wasn't far from the hotel, and b) it was much cheaper than Ruth Chris, and c) it was the only steakhouse the Groupon voucher was good for.

We ordered drinks, appetizers, and that couples

deal where two people eat off of one huge steak. Everything was perfect. At least it was until those Wild West Shrimp and seasoned steakhouse wings hit me. My stomach started rolling, and I knew trouble was brewing. My face had to have changed because Eric asked me if I was alright. I tried to play it cool, but my stomach was hurting so bad, I was starting to sweat. I told him we had to leave now, and the poor guy told the waiter to box everything up and bring the check.

When we got in the car, I told him my stomach was really hurting, and I needed to get to the bathroom. He had the bright idea that I just had gas, and I should stop trying to hold it in. Let's just say I learned the hard way that you should listen to the side effects portion of diet pill commercials. Apparently, fat blockers work by blocking all the fat or grease you eat from being absorbed. Guess who ruined her first date in forever by farting a grease slick into her panties? This girl. Guess who still isn't speaking to her husband because he laughed way too hard for way too long? This girl. Guess who is never taking fat blockers again? This girl!

Oily stool. Who knew? The only right answer to that is "not me." I'm calling them first thing Monday morning and reporting my refusal to pay due to dissatisfaction.

Dear Diary,

Let's just call today's session "Confessions of a Bad Christian." Sometimes when I read the Old Testament, I get jealous (and a bit angry, depending on what kind of day I'm having). The Israelites were just as bad as me. Worse even. Hell, I've never worshipped a golden calf, let alone did it shortly after God saved me—or at least I don't think I have—but for some reason, they get the awesome convenience of pillars of cloud and fire to show them the way. I know grace is better (in theory) and that I have the best gift in what Jesus did for me, but one also can't underestimate the importance of solid instructions. A little smoke signal during my next brainstorming session would be nice. Seriously, it would be. At any given moment, they knew exactly where they were supposed to be

while I'm over here feeling like I'm wandering in the dark half the time.

I know I can get instructions and wisdom from the Word, the Holy Spirit, and through prayer and fasting, but the fire and cloud just seems so much easier. But then again, they died quickly and en masse when they messed up. Maybe I should just shut up, stick with Jesus, and be happy about it. If I lived back then, I probably would have been smote . . . smitten . . . smitted? Whatever. Dead. I would have been dead.

Dear Diary,

I don't even know where to start. I feel like my mind is never off. Today, I asked my husband what he was thinking about, and he said, "Nothing." The worst part is I believed him. I asked him to teach me how he does that, and he laughed like he thought I was joking. I wasn't.

Sometimes I try to get decisions off of my mental plate by trying to gently delegate certain issues to him, but that always ends with him being fine with whatever I think. It's really not fair. Why should I have to carry the full responsibility for a bad call? Why should I have to be in a constant state of silent worry about how and when to do whatever? I want to sit down and think about nothing sometimes too. I'm starting to think "Hey, honey" is newspeak for "Hey, Thinker of the Things, think all of the things so I don't have to think anything."

Me: We have $300 left and $450 worth of bills; what do you think we should do?

Him: Whatever you want to do is fine.

Me: This is the problem. Here are three workable solutions. What do you think?

Him: Which solution do *you* think will work the best?

Me: I don't know (I always know); that's why I'm asking you.

Him: OK, well, whatever you think is cool with me.

Me: I don't want to choose wrong and you resent me for the fallout.

Him: It will be fine.

Me: … *dies a little more quietly inside*

I'm pretty sure this is how I lost my muchness. Silently dying tiny little deaths every day. I'm so tired of all this unnecessary dying.

Possible Solutions:

- ❖ Force him into action by refusing to decide anything.
  - ○ Complication: No decisions get made.
- ❖ Purposefully make bad decisions then parade the fallout.
  - ○ Complication: Who wants to self-sabotage their own family or finances?

- ❖ Stop talking to him about any and all decisions and just do whatever I want from the jump. He can either figure it out as he goes, or I could just give him directives.
  - ○ Complication: He suddenly feels emasculated and begins responding in a series of seemingly unrelated, passive-aggressive comments or actions.
- ❖ Keep doing what we've been doing.
  - ○ Complication: Continue dying tiny, silent deaths then turn into a raging Hulk monster fueled by the resentment that built steadily with every "Whatever you think is fine."

Dear Diary,

I. Need. A. Hobby.

Dear Diary,

Last night, me and the man I'm currently having trouble remembering why I married were lying in bed together. I farted, and this fool tucked and rolled out of the bed. Tucked and rolled! I mean, grow up, sir. Grow up.

Of course, after ten and a half years of marriage and four kids, you wouldn't expect a decent man to add insult to injury. But he did. After his acrobatics, he had the nerve, the audacity, the unmitigated gall, to ask me if I needed him to run me a shower. You fart a grease slick in your panties one time—*one time*—and they never let you live it down. Like it wasn't embarrassing enough to live through the first time. The worst part is he laughed so hard, I couldn't help but laugh too. Now, he thinks it's our thing. He's lucky divorces are expensive, and we are broke.

Dear Diary,

Another church was shot up today during service. I never thought I would live in a time where not even going to church is safe. The list of safe things to do for the general public is growing shorter and shorter with every news broadcast. At this point, people can't go to churches, concerts, stores, schools, parks, marathons, movies, galleries, work, corner stores, or gas stations. For us melanated folks, it's even worse. The odds of my husband being shot by a psycho in the movie theater is much lower than the odds that a rogue-ass cop will kill him during his next traffic stop.

It's enough to make you a recluse. How do you keep your kids safe in today's world? I almost feel guilty about bringing them into a place filled with so much darkness. I already haven't been feeling too positive about church lately. That shooting is

just the kind of thing that will make you feel justified in leaving and not going back. Per standard religious tenets, I should blame my feeling like that on the devil, but I'm pretty sure it's just me. I feel horrible for the families affected. I can't even imagine.

Dear Diary,

My baby growled at me today. Her brothers taught her how, and now she won't stop. The girl has two teeth and half a head of hair and got the nerve to be growling at folks. Part of me is like, "Yay, she's so smart, and it's cute that they play with her." The other part is like, "Oh dear, they are going to turn her into a monster." They also showed her how to do this cute little sniffy thing with her nose.

Speak of the baby, and it cries. Got to go.

Dear Diary,

The state of our finances is snowballing out of control. I nearly choked today when I realized how much we owe our mortgage company. Those half payments didn't take us nearly as far as I imagined. At this point, my husband is more likely to get laid off than get an hour increase, and I have no idea how we are going to catch up. I'm trying my hardest not to get overwhelmed, but it's not like I have anyone I can share the burden with. I need to figure out this mortgage thing while still maintaining the other bills. The thought alone makes me want to go into the living room and shove Eric's head into the YouTube video he's watching. OK, that may be excessive. I really need to find a healthy way to funnel my anger and negative emotions. I also need to come up with a plan for Kid Three's birthday early before I'm looking crazy

like I was for Christian's. Elijah's only going to be five, though. I can still get a whole lot over on him.

You know what? Instead of moping around stressed out about something I can't immediately control, I am going to hop in the shower and head to Bible study by myself. Outside of revivals, I never get to go to church alone. Just the thought of it sounds extremely peaceful. No fighting with the baby or fidgety kids. No picking baby snacks out of the seats and carpet. No nudging my husband awake at random points throughout the service. I may even take myself for a coffee afterward and a little stroll through Target. Buying a six-dollar coffee probably isn't the appropriate response to financially induced stress. But then again, what's six dollars when you need a few thousand?

Dear Diary,

I woke up today with the general feeling that everything will be OK. Nothing has changed, but I guess, for now, I'm cool with that because I feel like it will change. I don't know if it was church or the coffee. Either way, it's a relief.

I ran into Janice in Target. She asked me whose turn it was to host the kid-sit, and I told her I wasn't keeping track because I would no longer be participating. I think it may have come out a little harsher than I intended it to because she looked visibly shocked for a full five seconds before trying to convince me to not leave the group. A few months ago, I would have made excuses for my decision, but last night, I just told her trying to change my mind was a waste of time.

I wasn't trying to be rude to her, but the more she talked, the more I wondered how we ever became

friends. Being members of the same church for so long and having children close in age, I guess we gravitated to each other, but I realized that outside of those circumstances, I would never have aligned myself with her. This is deeper than her kid giving my kids the plague too. I realized I just don't like her . . . like, in general, as a person.

Dear Diary,

I figured it out! Since Kid Three's birthday is two days before Halloween, I am going to throw him a trick-or-treating party. I'll bake Halloween-themed cupcakes and set up a gift table. Everyone can meet at our house at six. We can trick-or-treat in a big group then come back and sing "Happy Birthday," eat cupcakes, open gifts, and *bam*, party over. No food, no favor bags, and barely any money spent.

I Googled cheap costume ideas, and this year, the whole family is going with a theme. Normally, each kid picks their own costume from Walmart or Target, but I just can't squeeze out twenty to thirty dollars a kid this time around. Me and Eric will be Mr. and Mrs. Pac-Man. All I have to do is cut two big circles out of cardboard and paint them yellow. Cut out the mouths, add some black construction paper eyes. Give Mrs. Pac-Man a little lipstick and

a bow and, *voila*, five-dollar costumes. The kids will all be ghosts. All I have to do is cut a head hole in the middle of a Dollar Tree tablecloth, glue on two big construction paper eyes, and throw it over a kid. It'll be adorable, but more importantly, it'll be economical. I'll need less than ten dollars to make costumes for the entire family. Sometimes I impress myself.

Dear Diary,

Today I bought my first pint of Borden's eggnog, and my life was all the better for it. My first thought was *Why is it out so early?* but as I placed it in my basket, I decided not to question God about His goodness. I should be thanking Him that eggnog is just a seasonal drink because if the stores sold it all year long, I'd be a shoo-in for a slot on *My 600-Lb. Life.*

Speaking of large things, when I walked in the store today, I was greeted by a giant inflatable Santa instead of a giant turkey. Halloween hasn't even gotten here yet and the stores are already setting up for Christmas. Clearly, they've forgotten that there is a whole holiday between Halloween and Christmas. Walmart is still not as bad as Hobby Lobby, though. They've had the Christmas stuff up since April over there.

Considering the way I'm feeling, maybe Christmas coming early will lift my spirits. Some good ole Christmas cheer may be just what I need. I should put the tree up early this year. The kids won't mind setting the tree up sooner than we usually do; they enjoy helping me decorate, but I don't think they care one way or another when they get to decorate. I may even spring for a real tree instead of the artificial one we drag from the attic every year. Tree shopping should make for a Facebook-worthy outing. Lots of cute pictures of the kids picking out their first real Christmas tree. This could be the beginning of a new family tradition.

I just realized I am not immune to marketing genius. I went from being upset about stores downplaying Thanksgiving to planning to put my tree up early in less than half a page because of a well-placed Santa inflatable.

Dear Diary,

Eric and I both keep saying that four is enough, and we don't want more kids, but I'm starting to wonder if that's really how we feel or if we just say it because we think (due to societal norms and opinions) that's how we should feel. I've noticed lately that we've been going back and forth with the occasional "guess it's time for one more" joke, and I can't figure out on a scale of 1–10 how serious we are.

The thought of having another baby is always fun, but the thought of living through another pregnancy and surviving another labor and delivery terrifies me. In a few months, I'll finally get my boobs back, and I'm not sure I want to give them up again. Not to mention the major production that is getting four kids ready for a hospital stay. That means finding someone I trust who is willing to keep all of my kids for an undisclosed amount of time while I'm in the hospital.

My husband refuses to go to work or home when I'm in the hospital so we would absolutely need a sitter. Unless . . . I give birth at home.

I would probably be temporarily devastated if I got pregnant and it was another boy. Fifty-fifty chances are a hard play to call. If it was another girl, it would be perfect. She could just share a room with her sister, and it would be fine. If it was another boy, we'd have to buy a bigger house or give up our master and throw two sets of bunk beds in there. Yeah, my vote is bigger house. Maybe my vote should be on not getting pregnant at all. Part of me is like, "Kids are too expensive" and "How can we afford more?" but another part is like, "Kids are a blessing from the Lord."

I wanted to be done having kids by thirty, so this last kid was timed perfectly. If I was going to have another baby, I would want to get pregnant tomorrow so the new baby could be close in age with Kizzy, but the thing is I don't want to get pregnant tomorrow.

Life is hard, and being an adult is confusing. A while back, somebody made a comment about how many kids I had, and it sent me into a journaling rant. My husband saying, "I guess it's time to make another baby," just sent me into another one. I wish I could say I want more kids or I don't want more kids and be confident in that choice. I wish I knew my own heart.

Dear Diary,

How embarrassing is it that my life is being controlled by a tiny army that I made myself? They've gone rogue, man, and I think the tiniest one is their leader. At this point, I feel like they are *actively* planning ways to ruin my day then taking turns executing them.

Score:

- ❖ Kids: 3,147
- ❖ Me: 6

Dear Diary,

I'm trying to work on not complaining so much, but I don't feel like it's working for me. My question is where do you draw the line between complaining and being honest? My entire life sucking right now makes that subtle distinction particularly important.

I'm sick of people telling me everything is going to be OK. Logically, I already know that, so hearing it just makes me want to scream. I'm just like, "Leave me alone and let me process my negative emotions in whatever way works or me." Being frustrated is not a sin. Punching you in the face because I'm frustrated probably is, though. As long as I'm not out here chopping people in the throat, let me be me for a minute. I almost hate to ask for prayer anymore because, in church, we get punished for thought crimes.

I know I'm supposed to think on things that are lovely, but goodness gracious, finding lovely things

to think on when your life is in shambles can be challenging. Just let me be challenged for a minute, for crying out loud! I'm skipping church tonight. I don't feel like doing the whole "It is well with my soul" song and dance. All is not well. I am not well, and church should be the one place where it's OK to admit that.

Dear Diary,

I can always count on a completely highlighted to-do list to lift my spirits. I was master doer of the things today. Too bad no one was here to witness it. I was a domestic ninja. Folding clothes while kids read to me. Cooking during their written work. I even read an extra bedtime story.

I wish I could experience the joy that is knowing Grover is the monster at the end of the book and still fully enjoying watching him panic until we get there. You know what? Come to think of it, I have known that joy. I read the entire *A Song of Ice and Fire* series (well, the ones George R.R. Martin has been gracious enough to finish at least), and I knew in my heart Jon Snow was really a Targaryen, but I still enjoyed every single moment up until they officially confirmed it.

Oh, God! That means my husband probably cringes internally every time I say, "Lets rewatch

Game of Thrones from the beginning" the same way I cringe externally every time the kids ask me to read *The Monster at the End of This Book* to them again. This right here is why journaling is vital: self-realization. I, Kayla Boudreaux, will not ask my husband to rewatch *Game of Thrones* again before season eight airs next spring.

Who am I kidding? Yes, I will.

Dear Diary,

What I wouldn't give for a five-day cruise to anywhere. Just me, the hubs, and several thousand strangers sailing into the sunset. At this juncture in our marriage, we only talk about the kids, and the majority of our sexual encounters take place in our bathroom or closet. The only upside is we are having more sex. I should stop there and say a short prayer, thanking God that our date-night-turned-Grease-Slick-Gate didn't damn us to an eternity without sex (insert praise dance).

I wonder if that grease slick was some kind of punishment for me wanting to have skinny sex in a real bed. If I was a guy and my wife spurted a grease gusher, I would probably never be attracted to her again. I acknowledge that that statement is equal parts horrible and true.

Anywho, back to how kids can make something

as simple as sex hard. I keep telling Eric that Kizzy needs to stay in her room now, but the first time she cries, he jumps up and gets her. He claims it's because he hates to hear her cry (oh, bless his bleeding heart), but I suspect he just doesn't want to risk me waking him up in the wee hours to go get her.

I never understood late-life divorces when I was younger, but now, I can see how after twenty years of co-parenting and quiet sex, you could look at your spouse and say, "I don't know you, and I'm not really sure if I like you." I don't want to become *that* kind of empty nesters, but I honestly can't remember the last conversation we had about something other than kids, work, or money. We do have the occasional conversation about salacious family gossip, but God in Heaven knows that is not enough to fuel a marriage. Date night died a slow, painful death due to a lack of funds and babysitters. In the spirit of marital revitalization, I thought it would be a good idea to get a few babysitter recommendations from other homeschoolers in the area, but that got me nowhere. One girl charged so much that my husband would have to work two hours to pay her for one. Her prices made me feel guilty about choosing not to work to stay home with the kids and, to be frank, a little guilty about having so many of the buggers.

I just want to eat a delicious meal that I didn't cook with my husband. No kids, no worries, no unfortunate fat blocker side effects. Just him thinking I'm cute from across the table. I really need to find a sitter.

Dear Diary,

I'm starting to feel like a big part of being an adult is realizing that we are probably going to spend a lot of time losing. My mom used to say, "I just can't win for losing" all the time when we were kids, and I never understood what it meant, but now, I get it. I mean, I still don't understand what it is actually supposed to mean, but I do understand that certain circumstances give you a burning desire to scream, "I just can't win for losing!" at the top of your lungs or whisper, "I just can't win for losing" into the rim of your wine glass. I may not *get it* get it, but I feel it right now.

I should Google the phrase and see what it actually means because it really doesn't make any sense. If I win, I didn't lose. If I lose, I didn't win. I'm not sure how to put that together in a way that makes sense at all. I give up. I just can't win for losing.

Scratch that last entry. I can win! Not only am I a winner, but I deserve a reward for being planner of the parties. I need a gold star for the financial genius that was "Trick or Treat Party." I spent less than twenty dollars on costumes and cake mix and barely another five dollars on décor. I grabbed two bags of Halloween rings from the Dollar Tree and stuck them on top of the cupcakes. Hobby Lobby had all their Halloween stuff for ninety-nine percent off because they have Christmas stuff all over, and boy, did I take advantage. It is amazing what you can do with two rolls of crepe paper and a package of cardboard cutouts. I painted everything black and orange and tossed black glitter around like my life depended on it. Elijah loved it, but then again, it's not hard to impress a five-year-old.

To top it all off, one of my horrible wife habits

came in handy. I was digging in the coat closet, looking for any extra Halloween decorations I may have tossed in there last year and found a bag of brand-new toys! Toys R Us tanked during the summer, and I went to their closeout sale back in June. I ended up spending more than I should have because everything was dirt cheap that final week. I must have tossed the bags in the closet to hide them from Eric. I found them neatly tucked under the bag of blankets we usually give to guests who sleep over.

I didn't realize I was covering them when I tossed the blankets in because I was fantasizing about choking out my sister-in-law with her constant nagging about my parenting choices. She better thank her lucky stars that I love my brother too much to flash out on her because there is nothing more infuriating than someone who doesn't have kids telling you what they would do with your kids as they silently, and not so silently, judge your parenting skills. I really pulled the short stick when it comes to sisters-in-law, but I digress.

The "party" was a hit, and our costumes said, "I'm a rock star domestic engineer who spends a lot of time on Pinterest" and not "We are foreclosure-on-the-horizon-level broke." The kids honored our long-standing, unspoken Halloween agreement without complaint: They give me first pick of all the good chocolate candies, and they get to eat themselves into a candy coma as long as no one throws up.

I spent the rest of the night eating mini Snickers, Reese's, Milky Ways, Kit Kats (who barely make the candy cut if I'm being honest), and those gooey Halloween peanut butter chews while watching *Grey's Anatomy*. After years of loving the show (except for when Izzy was sleeping with Brain-Tumor Denny), I think I've had enough. I forgave the loss of nearly the entire original cast. I forgave what they did to Derek after years and years of waiting for him and Meredith to get it right. I've been patient. I really have, but my God, I can't take a single 'nother gross love triangle. Of all the people you could write in, why, *why* would you try to make Deluca and Meredith a thing? Throw the whole show away! He's her sister's ex-boyfriend, for crying out loud. I don't know how much more I can take. It's bad enough that they waited until I finally stopped cringing every time Jackson and Maggie touched each other to put their gross little relationship on the rocks. The only couple I'm rooting for at this point is Teddy and Koracick.

Dear Diary,

Is it weird that I'm stressed out in advance about Thanksgiving's imminent descent upon my household? The only thing I love more than Christmas is Thanksgiving. Every year, I cook *everything.* The only things people are allowed to bring to my house are wine and a good appetite. If I had to guess, I probably spend hundreds of dollars every Thanksgiving. The money has never been an issue because a) my husband has no idea how much food even costs and b) because I enjoy cooking and baking that much.

Even if I start buying the stuff now, I still wouldn't be able to swing that kind of expense. It's not looking like Eric's hours are going to be increasing any time soon. I gently suggested he start looking for another job, but all he did was kiss me on the forehead and say, "It'll all be fine." "It'll all be fine" equals me grocery shopping for Thanksgiving dinner in the Dollar

Tree and hoping no one notices that my famous five-cheese baked macaroni was made with Dollar Tree cheese product slices instead. Throw the whole holiday away.

I'll have to put my thinking cap on for this one.

Dear Diary,

I was so anxious for my baby to start saying "mama." Then she said it, and I was so excited, and then she said it again. It was super cute, but in a dark, quiet moment in between those adorable, drool-filled syllables, I realized she will never stop saying it. I'll hear it through the crack under the bathroom door. I'll hear it through the sound of water running in the shower. I'll hear it through the clatter of pans every time I'm in the kitchen. I'll even hear it under the covers in the middle of bad thunderstorms.

It's the kind of blessing that makes you smile some days and cry others. To hear my daughter call mama a million times for everything and nothing will make me want to pull my hair out. But now that I've heard it, the idea of not hearing it seems so much worse. Loving your kids too much almost seems like a lose-lose battle, or a win-win. I'm not sure which. I love

my children ridiculously, but I also get tired of being mom-ed to death. Some days I feel like I'm being accosted by a different kid at every corner of the house. Can't live with them, but once you have them, you never want to live without them either. See what I mean? Moms can't win for losing.

Dear Diary,

Sometimes I feel like I'm suffocating. I just want to blossom into this amazing flower, but instead, I'm being choked out by weeds. How can I focus on secondary issues like purpose, goals, dreams, and ambition when I'm drowning in primary needs, like food or gas, what to pay, how to pay it, what kid needs what, what can wait, what can't, fix the car, fix the house, stay, go, burn it down?

I'm trying to be like Dory and just keep swimming. I really am trying to just keep going, keep pushing, but it's hard to stay positive in the face of so much adversity. I want to be a good Christian and just say all is well, but it's not. I wish people would stop telling me to let the joy of the Lord be my strength and tell me *how* to actually do that. I must be reading the Bible wrong or praying wrong or something.

Dear Diary,

I have no words for the chaos that was my life today.
None!

Dear Diary,

The other day, I saw a commercial for a new deodorant that you only have to apply once every forty-eight hours, and I was appalled. I thought, *Who in the entirety of all hell goes forty-eight hours without bathing?* That's two freaking days!

Now, let's fast forward to today. I lean in to pull clothes out of the washer, and the smell of hot armpit hit me in the face. I thought, *Surely, that can't be me*, but it was. After sniffing damp clothes and damn near everything else in the laundry room in an attempt to exonerate myself, I was forced to perform a self-evaluation.

- ❖ There was food on my shirt.
- ❖ There was baby spit-up souring on my shoulder (in my defense, I did wipe it off with a baby wipe when it happened, but it still stunk).

❖ My hair was unwashed, uncombed, and all around unacceptable. I mean, the worst kind of mom bun.

❖ My mouth tasted like stale coffee.

❖ I realized I hadn't showered in at least thirty-seven hours. I was mortified. Mortified and musty.

I thought, *My life is truly falling apart,* then, *If I had that new deodorant, my life would still be falling apart,* but *at least, I wouldn't be musty.* When did I go from being a twice-a-day shower-er and habitual bathtub soaker to the musty mama? I must have lost my impeccable standards of personal hygiene right along with my muchness.

Dear Diary,

According to Dave Ramsey, I need to start keeping my cash for different things in envelopes. That method should keep me from going over budget on household goods, groceries, eating out, and stuff like that. I'm hoping this will help me go from wasting $300 on what might be junk (organic or not) to spending just $100 on solid meals for the week.

It looks good on paper, but I can spend $100 in Whole Foods just buying organic fruits and veggies to make baby food.

Possible Solutions:

❖ Find cheap meals for large families on Pinterest.
❖ Start stripping.
❖ Stop feeding the kids . . . or the husband.

The way things are going, Cat is about to be eating leftover table food like a puppy.

Dear Diary,

I'm glad you can't talk because what I am about to say is so socially unacceptable that I would never say this out loud to another living soul. Judgement-free Zone: I almost throat-punched a kid today.

So I decided to splurge and buy myself a nice ChapStick. I picked out this cute little round lip balm and paid three whole dollars for it. I get home and my child picks it up off the dresser and asks to use it because his lips were dry. I told him no, to go use his Carmex instead, and I moved on happily with my life. A few hours later, I pick up my new, fancy ChapStick to put some on, only to find that he took a bite out of it. A real bite. I kid you not; he took a giant bite out of my brand-new ChapStick. I mean, what in the world would possess him to do that? And the worst part is I know he knew it was ChapStick. He made a

conscious decision to bite my brand-new three-dollar ChapStick.

I swear I had the burning desire to chop him in the throat. I literally thought about fighting him. What kind of human being thinks about punching a seven-year-old in the face? What kind of monster am I? I promise I could have tripped him or something. Instead, I just stood there fuming internally, and I'm pretty sure externally, as I listened to a chorus of "Wasn't me, wasn't me. Oh no, ma'am, it wasn't me."

Christian bit my brand-new three-dollar ChapStick then lied to my face about it. I don't know what's worse: the fact that I wanted to punch him or the fact that I didn't. Technically, I can't even prove the little monster did it.

I am clearly failing at this parenting thing. He may have won the battle, but I am going to get him back. I should start taking giant bites out of random things of his. I'm about to go bite a chunk out of his favorite foam football. He's never going to get a whole PB&J again.

Dear Diary,

I finally figured out Thanksgiving. I feel horrible about the solution, but desperate times call for desperate measures. I'm going to potluck it. I made a cute little invitation and sent it out in a group text. I figured since having to do anything other than show up would be a surprise for all of our regular attendees, I'd at least be courteous enough to give them as long as possible to prepare. The invite gave the date and time, along with a list of food items I would be providing. I asked everyone to bring the side of their choice and to RSVP their choices in the group text so we could avoid duplicates.

Hopefully, it'll go over well. I cringed as I typed every word. I just pray it didn't sound like "Bring food because I'm officially poor now." I guess anyone who thinks my request is tacky just won't come. I mean, it's not like what I'm asking is unreasonable.

I've paid for Thanksgiving by myself for years without complaint. They can contribute this one time. They should be happy, too, after all of those free meals.

I just don't want our family to think we are struggling, especially not my in-laws. Eric's family has no qualms about dropping little digs about me not working. They would revel in the fact that we're broke. It's sad when you can clearly tell which family members are just waiting for your life to fall apart so they can feel good about their own situation. My husband may be a procrastinating YouTube addict, but overall, he's still a good husband. Here's to hoping we won't have to relive the Easter Snafu of 2011. I told them then, and it's still true now, "I don't have to work or hide money because I'm not married to a selfish, lying, cheating, trash-ass asshole." That didn't go over well because two of his sisters and his mom are married to exactly that kind of man. Hit dogs holler and all that.

We eventually moved past it, but I know if they sense weakness, they'll be back on the attack. I cannot let them think we are not OK. They'll never shut up about it.

Realization: Why do I care what a bunch of miserable women in unhealthy relationships think about my family and what we may be going through? I worry too much about what other people think. I should figure out why that is then figure out how to stop.

Dear Diary,

My "probably not a real friendship anyway" with Janice has met its expiration date. In the spirit of Marie Kondo, it doesn't bring me joy, so it must go. Today, she called me to talk about Sarah and James, and I just couldn't take it. I'm not above some good tea, but I can't play with people who start their gossiping off with, "Oh, I'm so worried about so-and-so. I'm just telling you this so you know how to pray."

I'm stressed out enough without having to deal with other people's drama. We already know that James is not the best. I don't really need to hear about what asshole-ish thing he did today. Besides, Sarah and I are closer than Janice and me. I'd probably rank them both as associates. Well, Sarah is more of a friend than an associate. I don't know. But either way, I'm not going to sit down and talk about her

with Janice. Yes, she may be a horrible babysitter, but I chalked that up to her being pregnant and tired.

Oh, well. I have bigger fish to fry. These kids are giving me a run for my money.

Dear Diary,

I am starting to think my problem is I don't have any time to reset. I'm an introvert trying to be an extrovert, and it is causing me extreme mental and emotional distress. I realize I need quiet time away from people and their voices to start back at zero. You know, grounded and fresh. And that includes quiet time away from my kids. I am overwhelmed by voices and presences all the time because I'm surrounded by voices and people all the time. Be it the kids in my face while I'm trying to pee or people on the phone, I never have quiet alone time to wind down. I'm starting any given day at a five instead of a zero, and it's always a quick jump to ten from there. Starting my day at five is probably why my ChapStick getting bitten sent me over the emotional edge.

I need to schedule "me time," time I spend out of the house, alone, with no friends or phones. Just

quiet. On my husband's next day off, I'm going to sit in Panera Bread, buy a snack, and read a book. Now, I just have to make it until his next day off. Fortunately/unfortunately, that won't be very long since they still haven't increased his hours.

I feel like if I told this to another mom, they would be like, "I never get tired of my kids" or "I love them too much to need to be away from them." I mean, God knows I love my children fiercely. I've given up everything just to take care of them. I make baby food from scratch, for crying out loud. Needing to take care of myself doesn't make me a bad mom.

Mom guilt is a beast of a nature all its own.

Dear Diary,

There are some days you wake up and you just know there is a God. I mean, I know every day, but days like today, I *know* know. Between me and myself, I cried in the shower last night so no one would hear me. I felt like I could not go another day feeling these feelings or thinking these thoughts. Then, this morning, I woke up and God was here.

First miracle: I woke up before everyone in the house. I had time to read, pray, and shower before any of my kids got up. It was such a peaceful morning and a far cry better than jumping out of my sleep because a kid is:

* pulling up one of my eyelids
* asking for food
* crying because they peed the bed
* crying because they are already fighting

- ❖ crying because they woke up sick
- ❖ or my personal least favorite, being awakened by the silent, unsettling stare of a creepy kid

Like I said, act of God.

Then, I logged into the app to pay my light bill, and it was only $63.48. I was expecting, at minimum, $250. I searched the bill and couldn't, for the life of me, see where the credit came from. My bill has never been that low, *ever.* Had to be God.

It was a good day. No one called during school time, and we completed all of our scheduled assignments with no major upsets. There is no laundry to fold, and my house is clean. God looked at me crying in that shower and said, "That poor baby can't take a single 'nother bad day," and as usual, He was right. This day is probably the reason I won't snap and choke a kid out this week. I can't promise it won't happen in my mind, but keeping it from happening outside of my mind is what counts. The next time EJ is being obnoxious, I should look at him and say, "I thought about punching you in the face just now, but I won't because I'm a good parent."

There should be an award for not damaging the

little people you make with your own body in fits of child-induced rage. Moms do not give themselves enough credit. I feel like a ball of positivity right now. I should cry in the shower more often.

Dear Diary,

I. Am. Floored. Flabbergasted. I'm damn near speechless. Most importantly, I am utterly confused as to what course of action I should take.

So my husband comes home and tells me he saw James all chummy-chummy with another woman. My first question was "Why in the world didn't you take a picture?" But apparently, the thought never crossed his mind. I was wondering if she could have been a family member or coworker—you know, benefit of the doubt and all that—but Eric is convinced it was not. He said their behavior and interactions were very telling. He can't confirm that the guy is sleeping around, but kissing random chicks in public is still definitely cheating in our book. I'm pretty sure that's cheating in everybody's book.

I have no idea what to do. It's not like he and James are close. They are "our wives are cool" level

associates at best, so it seems weird to have Eric pull him aside about it. Part of me feels like going to Sarah and telling her what Eric saw, but there's no proof to really confirm what he said. I'm starting to think this is what Janice was trying to tell me the other day before I cut her off. I also don't have the energy or desire to call her back and play I-spy private eye.

Questions that need answers: Does bringing this info back to Sarah make me a bad friend, or does not bringing it make me a worse one? I feel like I'm torn between not wanting to be involved at all and feeling like the biggest fraud in the world if I'm around her pretending like I don't know anything.

Then, to top it all off, my husband had the nerve to go all "What would you want?" on me while we were talking about it. Honest answer: I don't know. I have no idea what my preference would be in that situation. I feel like if she was my best friend, I'd be at her door already with Vaseline, a baseball bat, a bag of sugar, and a handful of one-liners to shout out while we beat his ass. If she was a mere acquaintance, it would be easier to say, "Not my business." Unfortunately, Sarah falls in that gray, murky area where I care enough about her to not want to see her hurt or made a fool of, but I also don't know her well enough to know if this is the kind of situation that would make her kill the messenger.

I knew James was a bit of a douche and she was too sweet for him, but I didn't think he was "cheating on his pregnant wife" level douchey. I could really fight him in the street right now for a) being a cheating asshole and b) being sloppy enough for me to know about him being a cheating asshole.

I figured it out. What I'd really want in this situation is for my husband not to be cheating and putting the people around us in this predicament in the first place. I have no idea what to do. I feel like someone giving me that kind of info would just add embarrassment to the hurt and anger in a way. Would I want people to know? Hell, would I even want to know? I feel so bad for her.

Dear Diary,

Today we received a letter saying we have a ridiculously short amount of time to catch up on our mortgage payments or the remaining balance of our loan will be declared due immediately. My first thought was *If I barely have the $1,150 a month you want now, how in the entirety of all hell do you want me to pay the full amount?* Tell me, Mr. Banker Man, do you think I've been sending in late partial payments for months because I have $184,397.18 waiting for you in my back pocket? Under my mattress? In the bank account that your bank has charged me hundreds of dollars' worth of overdraft fees this year? I would have preferred if the letter just said pay or foreclose. At least that makes more sense than pay or pay much, much more.

My second thought was *You can have this raggedy*

mess of a house anyway because we can't afford to fix it anyway. We can just pack up, move away, and live the peaceful life of people with no mortgages or raggedy houses they can no longer afford.

My third thought was *Oh, crap!*

Dear Diary,

I was looking up ways to make money as a stay-at-home mom and starting a blog piqued my interest for about five seconds until I realized I don't have that kind of time. I need something that pays now. I can't do any of those call-based work-from-home jobs either. Every company I checked today had a strict no background noise policy, and that just won't ever fit with my bunch of monsters. I considered babysitting, but then I realized *I* still need a babysitter so I probably shouldn't be trying to be one.

Me majority of the time with my kids:

My kids + extra people's kids:

I'm going to have to vote no on anything that leads to smoke coming out of my ears.

I need to do something to take the financial burden off of my husband without upsetting our household dynamic because clipping coupons really ain't cutting it. Every time I see *Extreme Couponing*, I think it must be fake because there is not a single time my receipt or basket has looked like theirs. I would love to pay fourteen cents for $200 worth of household goods. But apparently, it's not in the cards for me.

Dear Diary,

Bad wife confession: I got that pre-foreclosure notice a few days ago and have been silently battling in my mind ever since. Part of me can't take the thought of watching my husband deflate right in front of me, and the other part is pre-angry at the possibility of him saying, "It'll be OK" and he's cool with however I want to fix it. My life is a mess.

He tries so hard. He literally has given all he has to provide for us. When we looked that first baby in the face and decided to teach him at home come hell or high water, we never even imagined the possibility of not having a home to teach him in. He knows we are behind and that things have been getting tighter since they started cutting overtime at the beginning of the year. But him not actively being involved in the handling of the finances has given him a peace that comes with never really knowing how bad things are.

His job cutting hours to barely full time put a bigger hole in an already sinking ship. He knows but in theory. Once I tell him this, he'll *know* know. I just don't want me saying "We're in real danger of foreclosing" to sound like "You suck as a man and have failed as a provider" to him. As much as I want to spare him that, I'm not sure how much longer I can shoulder this alone. I need to tell him tonight. Better yet, I'll tell him Friday. At least then he'll have a few days off to deal with his feelings and collect himself before he has to go back to work. That's the plan.

Dear Diary,

I dreamt that the sheriff dragged all of my kids out of the house so they could seize it. I've never been so afraid in my life. I woke up in a full sweat. I can't let my babies be homeless. I don't think I can wait until Friday to tell him. We need to start figuring this out now.

Dear Diary,

He cried.

Dear Diary,

Today, we stayed in bed with our kids all day. We watched movies and cartoons and ate pizza right in the bedroom. I'm going to have to Google how to get pepperoni grease stains out of my satin comforter, but my kids thought it was the coolest day ever. I even got a "You're the best mom" when I was tucking EJ in, and that kid is stingy with hugs and compliments.

I'm not sure how all of this is going to work out, but laying there snuggled up to my husband, I felt safe, like he would never let us be homeless. I felt like I didn't have to worry anymore.

Dear Diary,

Things I Googled today:

- ❖ Effects of antidepressants on breast milk
- ❖ Repossession laws for my state

Note to Self: Fix the garage door.

- ❖ How many movies has Samuel L. Jackson starred in?
- ❖ What do you do if your kid swallows a LEGO?
- ❖ Definition of the word "sallow"
- ❖ What is a short sale?

Dear Diary,

I finally put pen to paper, trying to work out our financial situation. I've come to the conclusion that we are screwed. Work hours are being cut, and expenses are on the rise. Between his lack of hours and the increase in our entire family's insurance costs, he isn't even clearing enough to cover bills and essentials, but somehow, he's making too much for us to qualify for any type of government assistance.

The food stamp office outright said no, and the cash assistance program told me they could not help me because I'm married. The bank said we can try a loan modification, but that it won't actually stop the foreclosure process, so that's pointless. Our mortgage payment increased a few months ago when our house insurance went up. We learned the hard way that house insurance is not actually meant to be used. File one claim on your shabby-ass house, and they

get their revenge at renewal time. That shouldn't even be legal, but here we are. Either way it goes, there is no amount of paperwork that will make them drop it back down now. I thought paying something was better than paying nothing, but it isn't.

Must-Haves:	Can Go:
✓ House	× Cable
✓ Car	× Amazon Prime
✓ Car Insurance	× Apple Music
✓ Lights	× ~~Netflix~~
✓ Water	
✓ Cell	
✓ Internet	
✓ Netflix	

The only other bills we have are the few low-limit credit cards I started applying for when our money first started coming up short. All this list did was prove that we have no wiggle room. I'll call in the morning to reduce our insurance coverage and our cell phone bills. It's not much, but it's a start.

Dear Diary,

I've been so consumed with my own life that I completely forgot about the whole Sarah/James scandal. Want to know what jogged my memory? Running into them in Target. It was the most uncomfortable moment of my adult life to date. I tried to escape before we were seen, but Eric just stood there looking like he was going to shit a brick. Neither one of us knew what to say, so it was all "Hey" and "Look how big they've gotten," which was especially awkward because we had just seen Sarah and the kids at church two Sundays ago.

Of course, we were punks, so we said nothing and hinted at nothing. Scratch that. We were smart and said nothing. What kind of monster tells a pregnant woman her husband is cheating in front of said husband, their gang of kids, and all the

happy Target shoppers in the baby section of all places?

Worst part: They invited us to their gender reveal. It's really a baby shower, but they don't want to say that because this is their fourth kid, and who throws a baby shower for their fourth kid? And, of course, their "gender reveal" is co-ed.

How is this my life?

Dear Diary,

Call us the great pretenders because I'm pretty sure we are going to have to fake it until we make it through Thanksgiving. I've been so mentally preoccupied that I forgot it was even coming. I have a jillion people planning to come to my house, and I have to cook everything I already said I would, all while hoping the sheriff doesn't show up to serve us a foreclosure notice in front of our entire family. I can hear the held back gasps of Eric's sisters already.

My husband thinks I'm worried for nothing because that probably won't happen. I said cops don't get holidays off, so it's possible—even if it's not probable—and, therefore, a legitimate reason to drink a glass (bottle) of wine.

Dear Diary,

Everything happens for a reason. Sometimes the reason is you're stupid and make bad decisions. I've never thought of myself as being stupid, but my recent predicament makes me want to re-evaluate that assessment.

Dear Diary,

Ask me no questions, and I'll tell you no lies, and since I'm not in a Pinterest positive mood, nor do I feel like beating the same dead horse with my metal bat of complaints, I've decided to just say nothing. I should've just skipped journaling today altogether. Dear God, if people find this in one thousand years, they are going to be convinced that women from this century were nuts. Or at least they'll think *I* was most certainly nuts.

In the spirit of not having a crazy, pointless rant with myself, I am going to slowly back away from the desk and go finish reading *A Handmaid's Tale.* Maybe Offred is having a better day than me.

Dear Diary,

My mama can be so annoying sometimes. This woman called me cockcrowing early, talking about she dreamt about fish. Seriously? A damn fish dream? Then, she had the early morning, wide-awake-with-no-coffee-drinking nerve to catch an attitude when I told her I don't believe in all those old superstitions.

"Every single time you've ever been pregnant, I've dreamt of fish, Kayla. Every time!" I told her she'd better call Man and Trell with that because this shop is closed for business. It can sure be their turn because I'm *done* done. Her old ass would not let up either. I told her when Man calls to tell us Latrell is the one who's pregnant, I'll be the one to throw their baby shower.

No matter what I said, she just kept on with it. I got off the phone by telling her I was going to put a drop of turpentine in a hot Coke so I could drink it

while hopping backward facing away from the sun and that I was going to spit on the broom on the way out the door for good measure, you know, just in case.

She was not pleased.

Dear Diary,

Thinking about my Thanksgiving shopping list just made me tear up slightly. I wish I could just skip to Christmas. Oh, dear God—Christmas.

I don't think there's enough pretending in the world to get me through these two holidays. If I hadn't sent the invites out so early, I could have canceled. Majority of our family members have already RSVP'd, so that's not an option now. My uncle is even coming in from out of state to see my mom. Maybe I could get them to host instead of us? I doubt my mama would want to take over, though. She stopped cooking for Thanksgiving as soon as I started, and I'm pretty sure that's a crown she does not want to pick back up. All she wants to do is eat then go to JCPenney with Dad so they can buy towels on sale.

If I ask my in-laws to host that kind of leaves my family out in the cold, and I just wouldn't give them the satisfaction. I think I'm trapped. I also think I'm about to go spike my eggnog.

Dear Diary,

I have washed the walls, dusted the bookshelves, scrubbed the baseboards, de-peed the kids' bathroom, cleaned the blinds, oven, microwave, and cabinets, and waxed the floors. Foreclosure looming on the horizon or not, I shall present nothing less to my guests than a shiny, dust-free homage to my amazingness as a domestic engineer. And besides that, the cleaning is not optional.

If a working mom has dusty blinds, it's because she's too busy doing important stuff outside of the house. She gets a pass. If a stay-at-home mom has dusty blinds, never mind her gaggle of kids, how long it actually takes to make, bag, and store organic baby food, or how time-consuming teaching said gaggle of kids can be, she is lazy. Lazy, inferior, and judged as such before a jury of her peers.

The sad part is if a working mom or a stay-at-home mom has dirty blinds, it's probably because they both hate cleaning blinds, and there is not a Pinterest hack cool enough to make dusting an enjoyable job.

Dear Diary,

Did you miss me? After days of cooking and cleaning like a madwoman, it is finally over. We had such an enjoyable holiday. Everyone who showed up had a side dish or a dessert—well, except for a couple of habitual free loaders we expected nothing from anyway. One of my cousins even brought an ice chest full of jungle juice. We had a blast. Only half of my in-laws showed up, but that just added to the day's appeal.

I will say that just when I start to forget how annoying Latrell is, she reminds me in spectacular fashion. She's lucky Man is my only brother and I want to keep him, so punching her in the face is a big no-no. Oh, but it's tempting. I can't wait until she has a gang of tiny monsters she made with her own body terrorizing her. I would love to be a fly on the wall

watching her implement all of that great, unsolicited parenting advice she stays giving me.

Fortunately for her, the sheer joy I felt from not having the sheriff show up and drag us and the turkey out kept me from saying that her lack of children made her grossly unqualified to direct my life concerning mine. I can't promise that I didn't imply it, though. Seriously, she corners me laying out the dessert table and gives me a freaking Ted Talk on phonics versus whole words and which way is the better route. I'm like, "Simmer down, kid, I've taught three children to read already. I got this." In the spirit of playing nice, I didn't say that. Instead, I smiled and said, "Oh, how interesting!" *sips wine* "Wow, I bet that was an insightful read," *swallows wine* "No, I haven't heard of (insert random child psychologist)."

I eventually excused myself to get a refill and joined another conversation. Well, not so much joined as watched. And there is nothing more entertaining than watching my dad and my uncle try to one-up each other on hard-knock-life stories. The kids ran in circles, Cat hid in a corner, and all was well with the world.

I had to finagle my way out of Black Friday shopping by giving a full monologue on the evils of commercializing holidays. "Why would I cut being thankful short to make it to the sales by five p.m.? So I can run some old lady down with my full belly for a discounted Blu-ray player?" I think I sounded convincing, but my mom gave me her infamous, sideways "I know you're full of it" look before they left. All in all, it was a good day. One major holiday down, one more to go.

Dear Diary,

Offred is gone, and I really wish I could know what happened to her. Unfortunately for me, I'm pretty sure if Margaret Atwood hasn't released a sequel in thirty years, it probably means she has no intentions of doing so.

I would definitely read *A Handmaid's Tale: After Gilead* or *A Handmaid's Tale: Life at Jezebels*. Hell, I'd even settle for *A Handmaid's Tale: Yeah, She's Dead.* Sometimes finishing a good book is like saying goodbye to a friend then never knowing how the rest of their life turns out. That feeling right there is the reason I love a good epilogue. *The Husband's Secret* and *An American Marriage* both ended the story then came right back in the epilogue and answered all of my nagging questions.

If I'm not homeless after the holidays, I'm going to try and find a local book club to join.

Dear Diary,

The toy ad from Walmart came in the mail today, and I am ashamed to say that I hid it . . . in the bottom of the trash can. Usually, I let the kids go through it and circle everything they want for Christmas, but this year, I'm not setting myself up for that kind of failure. Nope. Not doing it.

I'm going to shop the sales and get what I can afford for them. I need to set a per-kid budget and stick to it. I saw some ideas on Pinterest about economical gift ideas. One blogger said her kids each receive three gifts to represent the three gifts Jesus received from the wise men. Another said she gives her kids something to read, something to wear, something they need, and something they want. Both are clever ideas. I'll talk to the hubs and see what he thinks. Let me prepare myself for the impending "Whatever you think is fine."

Dear Diary,

Trouble is afoot. My mama called and invited me out for a cup of coffee. Problem: My mom doesn't drink coffee, and me and her have not been alone together in about ten to twelve years. Her and my dad are like the tag team of the ages. They never separate now that he's retired. They love each other's company so much that they never had empty nest syndrome or cried when me and my brother left.

They moved right into the "celebrating our freedom" phase and cruised to the Bahamas. The killer is after thirty-four years of marriage, they still seem perfectly content to be with each other *all the time*. I guess it's sweet in a sickly, annoying kind of way. Dad still ass-grabs her in public. It's disgusting, but I'll take that over the alternative. My in-laws divorced before their oldest kid made it out of elementary school, and they can't stand to be in the

same room. Every family event is a mental shuffle about which side to invite. It's always terribly messy.

Anywho, Mommy has summoned me, and I must go. I can't imagine what she needs to say to me alone. Hopefully, it's nothing concerning their health. I just realized, writing that last line, that my parents are as old as Methuselah. Mama calling solo may equal dad dying, which would suck because she wouldn't last a week without him.

What kind of dark and twisted things happen in my head that turned a coffee invite into certain death for both of my parents? I need therapy or medicinal marijuana. According to my budget, I'll have to settle for prayer, though.

Also, check on Jaz tomorrow.

Dear Diary,

Me: 7 ½
Kids: 1,267,993

I saw a video on Facebook that made my day. It showed me just what my life's biggest problem is.

- ❖ My problem: Pa-rent-ing
- ❖ The solution: A-phuken-brakE
- ❖ The leading cause of pa-rent-ing in my house: the fucking seven-year-old

Dear Diary,

My favorite thing about having a lot of kids is getting out of social interactions for lack of a babysitter. While I may cry many nights about not having a sitter for date night, I most happily waved my babysitter-less flag high when I got the reminder text about Sarah's gender reveal, a.k.a sneaky baby shower. Crisis averted. Awkwardness avoided. Don't you just love a good double-edged sword? Every con has a pro, and every storm cloud has a silver lining.

I'll just get a little gift and drop it off later in the week. I should invite her for lunch and use that as an opportunity to see where her head is at.

*Note to Self: Look up local lunch specials on Groupon.

Dear Diary,

It finally happened. A stern knock at the door and *wham*! We are in foreclosure. The sheriff's sale is set for three months from now, but it is my responsibility to continually check their webpage to make sure it is not moved up.

I visualized all my furniture strewn all over the lawn and immediately regretted not buying nicer stuff. Who wants old folks and vultures turning their bargain-sniffing noses up at kid-worn sofas and not-quite-crystal goblets? I just needlessly sent myself over the edge. Sheriff sale does not equal estate sale. I assume we can keep our stuff as long as we have it out before the sale date.

The level of panic that has arisen in my soul is so high that I think, as an act of self-preservation, my mind just shut my emotions off. I think the appropriate feelings for this situation are fear, panic, sadness,

embarrassment, and a crap load of anxiety. And I felt all of those things thirty seconds ago. It just dissipated into nothingness.

You know what? I quit. If my husband can't figure out how to handle this, then we'll just be up Shit Creek without a paddle because I just decided that I'm done being the fixer of the fucking things and the bearer of the bad news. I'm not even mentioning it to him. I'll leave the notice on the dresser, and he can figure it out whenever he notices it.

I am going to teach the kids, watch trash TV, and snack until my poor little heart is content. He can fix this thing, and I should tell him duct tape and nails won't work. Better yet, I'm not even telling him that. I'm off to enjoy the rest of my day.

Dear God,

Please forgive me for lying to my mom. After yesterday, I couldn't handle her fun-filled outing or whatever potentially horrible news she's harboring, so I got out of our coffee date by telling her I had a sick kid. I knew the words "stomach virus" would buy me at least a week delay on our little chitchat. Worked like a charm, but now I feel slightly guilty, more about lying on my kid than lying to her if I must be honest. If Elijah gets sick for real, I'll probably never let myself live it down.

I've done nothing so far today but lie to my mother, and I feel like I need a nap already. I'm pretty sure I'm going to cancel school for today. Watching a little television won't kill them. I remember days at school when we watched movies all day, and it still counted. I'll make them throw in a documentary and some phonics videos and call it a day. I deserve a small break anyway.

Dear Diary,

Eric still hasn't read that notice. Sometimes I'm amazed at how completely oblivious he can be. My aggravation is about to turn into downright disgust. I'm just here. Seething. One would think he would be able to smell the frustration seeping out of my pores like pheromones or animal musk. But no. He's just as happy-go-lucky as can be. I almost feel like he's forgotten that we are in a serious bind. He has probably just assumed I have it taken care of. I can't even blame him for that, seeing as I've literally solved every problem we've faced single-handedly with nothing more than his "Whatever you think, babe" for the past ten-plus years.

I, however, would think that the lack of full course meals, the fact that he ran out of clean work shirts today, and the fact that our floor hasn't been mopped

in days should have alerted him to the fact that I have given up my post as doer of the things. I'm about to grab a bottle of wine and enjoy no longer being the feeler of the feelings.

Dear Diary,

I think I've finally lost it. Better yet, I'm pretty damn sure I did, and I have no idea how to get it back. Today, I stalked my house like the beast from *Split*. I devoured every pure thing in my path and savored the taste of their fear. I was personality #24.

I haven't had a mothering fail this bad since my brief stint as third-trimester mommy. I punished, I spanked, I ranted and raved, I trashed toys and movies left out on the floor. It was horrifying. My emotions had free reign, and they drove me far and fast. I went from loving, encouraging teacher to critical monster. I turned into Samuel L. Jackson right in the middle of my kitchen, and I mean full-blown Sam L. Elijah was teary eyed, the baby was screaming, EJ looked like he was teetering between horror and disgust, and Mr. Chapstick Eater just stood there smiling and storing away new, fun curse words for future

reference. When Eric tried to intervene, I turned on him. I was the worst kind of one-woman show, and today was not the day I would have wanted Jesus to knock at the door.

I just felt (and still feel) full of rage. I wanted to destroy everything in sight. My poor kids. My poor husband. I feel horrible. And not regular horrible either. I'm talking the kind of horrible that makes your stomach upset. I don't know what's wrong with me.

I haven't been reading my Bible or having focused prayer. To be honest, I can't even remember when the last time I even talked to God was. I think I'm mad at Him. Better yet, I am mad at Him. And even worse is the fact that I feel like I have every right to be mad. In my mind, I know God is never wrong. In my heart, I'm pissed that He even let it get to this. Our situation is a blend of uncontrollable circumstances and a whole lot of poor financial decisions, but sometimes I just wish God would stack the deck in our favor.

I feel hopeless and broken, and I'm so angry that I don't even want to ask for forgiveness. I want to give God the silent treatment. I feel like my crazy is at a point of no return.

Dear Diary,

I tried to Google what's wrong with me, and after a series of symptom-laden articles and internet quizzes, I've discovered that I am:

- bipolar
- OCD
- suffering from postpartum depression or post-partum psychosis
- having thyroid issues
- possibly schizophrenic

Apparently, there are no essential oils for any of this. I hate the internet. I'm going to bed early tonight. Melatonin for everyone.

Dear Diary,

You know what? Never mind.

Dear God,

I'm sorry I'm so upset with you. If it makes You feel any better, I'm mad at my husband too, even though, logically, I know it's not his fault either. I need forgiveness, healing, and a really good therapist. Please break the stronghold these negative emotions have on me. Help me feel right things, think right things, and do right things. This feels like the kind of thing that requires fasting and prayer. Help me.

P.S. God, forgive me for being financially irresponsible over the years. Give me wisdom.

Dear Diary,

I don't have the words to describe this day. Correction: I have so many words to describe this day that I don't even know where to start. I am dumbfounded. Seriously. I have a cry caught in my throat, and I feel like I'm choking on it.

I finally met my mama for coffee, and I could not have guessed how this conversation was going to go. She started off with her usual "How's life, the kids, the husband?" spiel and I responded with the usual lies, "Good, great, all is well." Her reactions were painstakingly pleasant. None of her sly homeschooling remarks or subtle mediocre husband digs. I fully expected the small talk to segue into something involving the words "stage four," but she never got to it. She just kept asking about the kids, the husband, and the house. I literally ran out of ways to say it is well.

I tried to feign interest in my bagel and made a

small fuss over my coffee, but nothing deterred her. Kids. House. Husband. Kids. House. Husband. Kids. House. Husband. I was so desperate to stop her onslaught of questions I would never answer honestly that I considered dropping my hot coffee in my lap because at least then I could rush home to change or be taken to the emergency room for third-degree burns to my va-jay-jay. Both outcomes would have effectively changed the topic of conversation, so I was good with either.

Just as I was sliding my mug to the edge of the table, my mama called me a liar. Not in a loud, rude way but in a sad, disappointed way. Rude mama I can handle. I've grown a thick skin for her, but disappointed mama is a whole 'nother monster. And that monster ripped a piece of my heart out and tossed it into my coffee cup.

After a brief monologue about how she raised me and that I'm never too old to trust and confide in her, she asked again. Kids. House. Husband. I am a tad bit embarrassed to admit that I bawled. In lieu of responding like an adult, I cried like a baby right there at the too-small coffee shop table. And I mean snot and booger tears. It was so undignified. I'm not even sure how she understood what I was saying through all the snorts and wheezing for air. I cried so hard that it gave me a headache. I told her about the house, how horrible I'd been to the kids lately, my desire to divorce God and my husband, and how I feel like I'm losing my mind. I didn't even notice when she got up and wrapped her arms around me.

There is something oddly comforting about the smell of White Diamonds. But that could be because it's the scent of every hug my mother has ever given for as long as I can remember. I'm not sure how long I held onto her, but when I unburied my wet face from her sweater, her checkbook was on the table. Her next question was how much. That brought more tears. After several minutes of me protesting, she pulled her mommy card and wrote what she wanted.

Apparently, her and Dad have always put money aside for me and Man. The money was initially meant for college, but James "The Golden Boy" Jr. broke their hearts when he decided not to go, and I had scholarships. After that, it transitioned from school money to whatever money: weddings, home down payments, or whatever we would eventually ask for. Problem is I'm so prideful that I never asked for any-thing. When I couldn't afford the wedding I wanted, I eloped. They didn't even find out we were buying our house until we invited them over after we final-ized all the papers and got the key.

To ease my embarrassment, she even told me that a few months ago, my dad had taken my brother out for drinks and gave him $15,000 to help pay for one last round of fertility treatments. She said Man and Latrell have been trying for years to conceive, and they can't afford to try anymore. I tried to buy myself some time to process by telling her I could not accept that type of loan without speaking to my husband about terms and making sure we could repay them in a reasonable amount of time. Then, she turned into Sam L.

In the end, I left with a check that was meant to pay for me to backpack through Europe during college, help buy my first house, or whatever I had desired if only I had asked.

I came home thinking, *I'll lead with "It's a gift"* when I show the check to my husband, but now, I'm thinking I won't show him at all. I should just clear up the foreclosure and let him think we are going to be homeless for a few weeks. Like a social experiment, the results of which would likely lead us straight to divorce court.

I don't know how to respond to my parents or my husband right now. "Thank you" just doesn't seem to cut it, and "Honey, everything is fine now" doesn't feel like the right option either. I said thank you a gazillion times at the coffee shop, but it feels inadequate for the level of saving-my-entire-ass my parents just did. I've always thought my parents were OK financially, like "you can be comfortable as long as you budget your retirement checks" OK, not "pensions and a lifetime worth of CDs and savings" OK. And to think I thought them paying for a tablet was a strain on their fixed income. I think I'm going to sleep a little more peacefully tonight. I'll deal with the husband tomorrow.

Dear Diary,

I still have not dealt with the husband. I spent the day aimlessly scrolling through Facebook and Pinterest. It felt so good to spend a day without constant worry running in the back of my mind like a default program. My life is clearly turning around, and I know it because today, I saw an article saying that after, thirty-plus long years, Margaret Atwood is finally releasing a sequel for *The Handmaid's Tale.* It felt like God's little way of telling me He wants to be friends again.

Dear Diary,

I'm so annoyed with Eric. Even though I know our financial problems are solved, he doesn't, and I can't understand, for the life of me, how something as serious as potential homelessness is still whatever-you-likable to him. What is the point of being married if you still have to do all the hard stuff alone? If the pre-foreclosure notice didn't light a fire under him, being served should have.

He has not offered a single suggestion concerning our predicament. He hasn't so much as offered to stand in prayer together about it. I mean, I hadn't been in a praying mood anyway, but it's just the principle. If he came home and said, "Let's start a meth lab," I'd consider it an improvement on him saying and doing nothing. I've seen *Breaking Bad*. Meth doesn't seem very hard to pull off. I'm just saying.

I called the bank to find out their preference of

payment type to catch up our mortgage, but they said we have to go through the lawyers now since we are in foreclosure. I should be getting a letter within the next few days outlining everything we have to pay, including the past-due mortgage balance, late fees, and the lawyer's fees attached to our account now. Me and the chick at the bank got into a full-blown argument because a) when I say "Take my money," just take my damn money! Who makes it difficult to collect something they've been fussing to get for months? It was infuriating. And b) she had an attitude about sending me a full statement because she claims she already sent us one. I almost lost it. I wouldn't have thrown that away or not read it, so I know that wasn't true. She kept insisting until, finally, I told her it didn't matter if she *thinks* she sent me one thousand copies, if I requested another one, just do your damn job and send me another one. People clearly don't vet their customer service employees before they hire them anymore.

On another note, I tried to express my gratitude by sending my parentals a huge Edible Arrangement, thanking them again for their help. My dad texted me a smiley face emoji. My mom's text just said, "Stop wasting money." I guess she has every right to tell me to stop wasting money since it was her money. I'm going to get them some extravagant Christmas gifts and see what she texts then. I'm so excited that I get to enjoy Christmas now. After this quick paperwork shuffle, we will be free and clear. No sheriffs dragging us out in the snow we won't get because who am I kidding; this is the South.

I guess the Big Toy Book can come out of hiding. Aw, dammit. I can't have Christmas without my stupid-face husband. I'll deal with him tomorrow.

Dear Diary,

I still can't deal with the husband. I've tried, and I can't. Cannot. *Caaan't!* Every little thing he does sends me so far over the edge that I can't even talk myself down anymore. My response to everything he does now is over the top. It's like I'm at a ten when I want to be at a two. I can't talk to him about the money or the foreclosure because at this point, I can't even get through simple pleasantries.

If I knew for sure that I had a faithful enough friend who was financially stable enough to send me cigarette money regularly, I'd just off him. The sad part is I'm not even sure how serious I was about that. He is pretending not to notice the sharpness of my responses or the way I readjust myself when he walks by to avoid even the accidental grazing of his body against mine. His passive aggressiveness just makes me angrier. I literally caught myself snarling at

him through a fake smile because the kids were in the room, and I didn't want to be the crazy angry girl in front of them. Afterward, I felt like that probably made me look crazier and angrier.

My responses to his actions are completely disproportionate, and I don't know how to make it stop. I keep hearing those proverbs in my head about living with a contentious woman and how a foolish woman will tear down her house with her own hands, and I feel like that's the Holy Spirit telling me to sit down, shut up, and play nice. God knows I don't have a "sit down and shut up" spirit. And as soon as I decide, "OK, I'm going to play nice," he breathes too loudly as he walks into the room, and I am right back over the edge. I feel possessed, like I'm watching myself be crazy but have no power to control it.

He forgot to put the garbage to the road on trash day, and I threatened divorce because if I have to do everything myself, I might as well be alone. He farted in bed, and I jumped up in a full rage monster fit, raving on and on about how inconsiderate and disrespectful he is. In my defense, it was bad. I mean horrific. He must have eaten ice cream with the kids or something.

Today, he asked if I would like to go out to dinner, and I lectured for thirty minutes about how financially irresponsible and negligent he was because if he helped with the budget like I asked or at least listened when I spoke, he would know that we don't have out-to-dinner money. I then stormed out of the house and snuck off to eat a Chipotle burrito bowl in the car with a large slush from Sonic.

I need to make it stop. I have never been this upset with another human being in the entirety of my life. It tastes like blood and metal in my mouth. I'm choking on the vilest things I want to say because, thank God, I haven't quite reached the level of degradation required to stoop that low yet. I promise I'm <----> this close to talking about his grandmama. The worst part is while logically I know I'm wrong, emotionally I feel like he deserves it. Like he should feel externally the pain he's forced me to bear alone internally. I'm a monster.

Dear Diary,

It felt so good to get the kids out of the house today. Malika met me at Sky Zone with her gang, and we turned the little monsters loose. Our kids haven't played together outside of church since Elijah's trick or treat party, so they were beyond happy to see each other. Sky Zone isn't our usual stomping ground, but it was too cold for the park, and Chuck E Cheese has been banned since the attack of the animatronics. It felt good to be able to enjoy my kids enjoying something without stressing about what bill I didn't pay for them to enjoy it. It felt even better to be able to talk through what I've been going through with an adult. Hell, at this point in my life, talking to any adult in person about anything is amazing with the amount of time I spend trapped in the house with all these kids. I fought tooth and nail to pay for all the kids to jump and ordered them pizza for lunch. Malika

wasn't going for it, but eventually, she saw reason and relented.

I was a little embarrassed to tell her about Eric's hours being cut and how we'd fallen behind on the mortgage. She just sat there, looking judgement-free when I told her about the foreclosure and what happened with my mom. I don't really know what I expected her response to be. I guess me talking to her about it was more about me needing to get it off my chest to someone other than my mom than it was about her actual response. Sarah would have hugged me and tried to make me feel like everything would be OK. Janice would have feigned compassion then called our other mom friends one by one to tell them everything under the guise of "We should really lift her up in prayer." Malika just listened. When I finished talking, she told me that everyone goes through rough times. Her and her husband had to file bankruptcy a few years back to stop their house from going into foreclosure. She said her husband made a mistake on a job that caused his company to lose their best customer. After he was fired, they had to live off of his unemployment, which was pennies, for months. She had to apply for food stamps and Medicaid.

I felt horrible that she went through that, and that

none of us noticed. But I guess I shouldn't because no one noticed that we've been struggling. It was all kumbaya and support until I told her that I still hadn't told my husband about the money and that I'm pretty sure if I can't adjust how I'm feeling and, more importantly, how I'm treating him, I'm probably headed for divorce. At that point, sweet, supportive Malika called me an asshole and told me to get my shit together ASAP. I couldn't even be mad because she's right. I told her I would try. I'm not sure how far that will get me, though, because I've been trying. I don't know. I guess I'll try harder.

Dear Diary,

I finally got the statement Mrs. Did Not Want to Do Her Job sent out. After I pay the back mortgages and extra fees, I'll still have $2,753.69 left over from the parentals money. Well, I guess it's my money now. I'm going to cash that check tomorrow and get a cashier's check and send it to the lawyer handling the foreclosure. Once that's done, I can officially begin Christmas shopping because there is nothing lonelier than a fully decorated Christmas tree with not a thing underneath it. I told the kids Santa didn't have enough elves to start dropping gifts off early like he usually does. I'm pretty sure that dang nine-year-old doesn't believe in Santa anymore, but a good eye cut and a well-placed "You can't get gifts from someone you don't believe in" was enough to keep him quiet.

Dear Diary,

It's really annoying to be married to a saint. Instead of beating me or cheating on me or divorcing me for being a monster lately, my husband just called and said his mom is on her way to watch the kids because he set up a really nice spa day for me. When she gets here, I'm supposed to go get a mani-pedi, a massage, then get my hair done.

My instructions are to buy something nice to wear and report home by six so he can take me to dinner when he gets off. I must say, I still hate him with the fire of a thousand burning suns right now, but I guess I can play nice for a day of pampering. I should cut all my hair off so I can enjoy watching him secretly hate my new short hair while being too passive aggressive to actually say he hates my new haircut. No, what I should do is take Malika's advice and try to not be crazy, seeing as I can't even

remember the last time we had a real date night. Never mind, yes I do.

Note to Self: Avoid greasy food just in case God is in a joking mood.

Dear Diary,

I don't judge books by their covers, and apparently, I shouldn't judge people either.

List of People I Secretly/Not-So-Secretly Owe an Apology:

- ❖ My husband
- ❖ My brother's wife
- ❖ The lady from the bank
- ❖ The guy I flicked off in traffic yesterday for honking at me (I did cut him off)
- ❖ My kids
- ❖ God
- ❖ The grocery store clerk (my coupons were expired)

List of People I Actually Will Apologize To:

- ❖ God
- ❖ My husband

I owe God an apology for being so sinful and horrible. I was mad at Him and the world, and I couldn't even pull myself together enough to pray about it. Fortunately, I know He loves me, crazy and all, so we cool.

I owe my kids an apology for being a full-blown monster mommy recently. I've just been so tired and irritable lately. That's not an excuse either, more of a statement of fact. Hopefully, I haven't said or done anything that causes permanent emotional damage and forces them into years and years of counseling to fix what I broke. Kids are resilient, though, so I'm sure they'll be fine. I'll take them out for ice cream and explain that my behavior toward them and their dad has been wrong, then I'll ask for their forgiveness.

I owe my husband an apology because I've spent the last few weeks making his life a living hell every chance I got. I cut my hair to spite the man, for crying out loud. I felt justified in doing so because I honestly believed he had dropped the ball, but I was wrong on both fronts. As soon as he saw the foreclosure notice on that dresser, he called the bank to see what we could do to stop the foreclosure, and the bank lady sent him all the appropriate paperwork and instructions on contacting and dealing with the lawyer, handling the foreclosure on their end. She wasn't lying to me (hence the apology she needs but will never get because I can't remember what her name is). Once he received that info via email, he contacted the lawyer and found out it would take close to $4,000 more than what we actually owed to stop the foreclosure once they included all the late fees and lawyer fees.

Then, the husband, who I thought was doing nothing, thinking nothing, or worrying about nothing, battled with his 401(k) to get an emergency withdrawal. We're still paying on the loan we took out two years ago, and they won't let you have more than one loan out at a time, but if you can prove the emergency (which he did by sending them the foreclosure notice), then they'll let you make an early withdrawal that doesn't have to be repaid. The downside is he was penalized severely for the early withdrawal, and we have to claim it on our taxes as additional income, all of which I think is a *scam*, but I digress. All in all, it was a good idea. He has plenty of time until retirement to build it back up, and to be honest, who can really worry about the future when you are trying to survive today? He got the check day before yesterday and decided a day out and dinner was just the way to surprise me with the information.

I was elated until he told me that the reason he didn't tell me any of this up until now is because he didn't want to stress me out with me being pregnant and all. I lost my whole mind right then and there. (Also, on the list of reasons I need to apologize to my husband). He said me being volatile, permanently fatigued, and overly emotional are classic "You're about to have a baby" signs. Him ignoring my outbursts and being really nice while I was being obnoxiously mean was because he thinks there's an alien lifeform controlling my reactions from my uterus.

I told him that I am *not* pregnant and that I was upset because I thought he was doing nothing about the foreclosure. And by told him, I mean told him and half of the restaurant patrons. He started laughing, and I started crying. When I looked up, he said, "Yeah, you're definitely pregnant."

Clearly, I must be fatter than I think, which is horrible because I think I'm pretty fat. I probably should have apologized to him over dinner, but I went from being so happy about him actually doing the things to being so upset about the pregnancy comment that it didn't even cross my mind. I didn't even tell him I'd already paid the lawyer. I'll definitely talk to him about that when he gets off before he pays them too. I should tell him sorry too because I really am. Or maybe I'll just have sex with him. He'd prefer the sex. Apology out. Sex in.

Things to Do:

- ❖ Set up thank you dinner with my parents per husband's request. (Even though I really think he just wants to tell them that he already had it covered.)
- ❖ Double-check the last time I took my Depo shot
- ❖ Don't panic.
- ❖ Don't panic.
- ❖ Don't panic.
- ❖ Buy the damn Christmas gifts before you for-get . . . again.
- ❖ Pick a new birth control, like yesterday.
- ❖ Buy a new journal.
- ❖ Don't panic.

Dear Diary,

I have scoured my Happy Planner to see when I last took my Depo shot. It literally has everything in it. All of my things. Its full of lists of things to do, things done, things I want to do, things I didn't do, so for the life of me, I can't understand why I didn't write any birth control things.

Who mishandles such a major area of their life? Stupid people, that's who. Everything happens for a reason, and sometimes the reason is you're stupid and you make bad decisions. I haven't had a cycle, but I think that's normal when you've been on the Depo shot.

Two things: One, join a gym. I will not have people giving me their seats on the bus because they think I'm too pregnant to stand. I'm never actually on a bus, so that particular situation will never happen, but the underlying point is still valid.

If I've gotten so fat that the guy who sees me naked thinks I'm growing a baby, that's a problem, a problem only dwarfed by the chance that I may actually be growing a baby. The aforementioned gym can help with the problem of looking pregnant when you are not, but I guess, first, I have to know that I'm not. Two, take a pregnancy test. Scratch that. Two, drink a glass of wine. Three, then take a pregnancy test.

Acknowledgements

There are many people who deserve thanks for supporting me on this journey to bring *Dear Diary* to life. First and foremost, my husband, whose literal support allowed me the freedom to write (or not write) full-time—just joking; I have four kids; the only thing I do full-time is fuss, but his support has definitely given me the freedom to write when I want to. He also never laughs when I tell him my newest book ideas (even though some of those ideas have been totally laughable). I am grateful for my little sister, Kelia White, who believed in my idea to create a fictitious journal about a stay-at-home mom from the beginning. She was the first person to read, critique, and encourage me to get my *ish* together and get this book out to the world.

Publishing *Dear Diary* would not have been as easy or enjoyable as it was for me without Monique D. Mensah and her entire team at Make Your Mark Publishing Solutions. Because of them, I am able to present a book that I am proud of to the world. After the horror story that was my first publishing experience, it was refreshing to work with someone who was professional and passionate about making my book into a masterpiece.

Sincerely, I would like to thank everyone who helped fund *Dear Diary* by giving to my Kickstarter campaign. Without the support from Phil White Jr., Ivy Sias, Matthew A. Cherry, Tyra Davis Brown, Sable Bourgeois, Althea Jenkins (aka Aunt Judy), Latoya Smothers, Megan Wooding, Stephanie Brooks, Pansy St. Julien, Sharika Olivier, Inga Patterson, Danika Denise Duhon, Patrice McCullum, Erin Nkele, Ryan M Campbell, Tracy Daniel, Brittney D. Ball, Ibrahim Muhammad, Megan Manuel, Unique White, Brittany Manuel, Simone Green, Ashley McNeil, Chasity Caesar, Jermey and Shani Nelson, Liara Tamani, Megan Begin, Sarah Jensen, Casey Dugas, Monifa Mccarther, Azia Davis, and Laina Bell *Dear Diary* would not be in readers' hands today. I am eternally grateful.

Thank you for reading *Dear Diary*.
If you enjoyed this book, please help spread
the word by leaving an online review.

KEEP IN TOUCH WITH KEVIA DAUPHINEY
Website: www.keviawrites.com

Faebook: https://www.facebook.com/keviawrites

Instagram: @keviawrites